D0174029

"You shouldn't be [...] **the person who killed your student and tried to abduct you," Matt said.**

Claire shook her head. "I'll be fine. I was just in the wrong place at the wrong time. No one is after me."

"We don't know that, Claire. You could still be in danger."

She glanced up at him, curiosity pooling in her eyes. "Why? What did you find?"

"Your student, Luke, didn't send you that text asking you to come to the school. He couldn't have. He was already dead by the time that text was sent. Whoever it was lured you here and was waiting for you, Claire."

He saw her mind racing. "Who would do that? Who would want to hurt me?"

"That's a good question, and one we need to figure out." He'd meant it when he'd said he wasn't leaving until he knew Claire was safe...and that was looking less and less likely. There was no way he was going to let her go home alone. She would be a sitting target. "I would feel better if you weren't alone."

She gazed at him for a moment. Was she thinking of the past?

Virginia Vaughan is a born and raised Mississippi girl. She is blessed to come from a large Southern family, and her fondest memories include listening to stories recounted around the dinner table. She was a lover of books from a young age, devouring tales of romance, danger and love. She soon started writing them herself. You can connect with Virginia through her website, virginiavaughanonline.com, or through the publisher.

Books by Virginia Vaughan

Love Inspired Suspense

Rangers Under Fire

Yuletide Abduction
Reunion Mission

No Safe Haven

REUNION MISSION

VIRGINIA VAUGHAN

HARLEQUIN® LOVE INSPIRED® SUSPENSE

If you purchased this book without a cover you should be aware that this book is stolen property. It was reported as "unsold and destroyed" to the publisher, and neither the author nor the publisher has received any payment for this "stripped book."

Recycling programs
for this product may
not exist in your area.

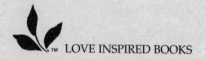

™ LOVE INSPIRED BOOKS

ISBN-13: 978-0-373-44738-1

Reunion Mission

Copyright © 2016 by Virginia Vaughan

All rights reserved. Except for use in any review, the reproduction or utilization of this work in whole or in part in any form by any electronic, mechanical or other means, now known or hereinafter invented, including xerography, photocopying and recording, or in any information storage or retrieval system, is forbidden without the written permission of the editorial office, Love Inspired Books, 195 Broadway, New York, NY 10007 U.S.A.

This is a work of fiction. Names, characters, places and incidents are either the product of the author's imagination or are used fictitiously, and any resemblance to actual persons, living or dead, business establishments, events or locales is entirely coincidental.

This edition published by arrangement with Love Inspired Books.

® and TM are trademarks of Love Inspired Books, used under license. Trademarks indicated with ® are registered in the United States Patent and Trademark Office, the Canadian Intellectual Property Office and in other countries.

www.Harlequin.com

Printed in U.S.A.

Yet, O Lord, You are our Father. We are the clay,
You are the potter: we are all the work of Your hand.
—Isaiah 64:8

This book is dedicated to my mom, Sylvia.
Your strength and perseverance throughout the years
has been my inspiration. God truly blessed me
when He made me your daughter.

ONE

Claire Kendall unlocked the side door to Lakeshore High School and slipped inside. The hallway was dark and eerily quiet on a Sunday afternoon. The hall lights were controlled by a main switch in the storage room, but they took a while to power on and Claire didn't want to bother with them. The overhead light in her classroom would be enough, especially if she opened the window blinds and let the sunlight stream in. She took out her cell phone and hit the flashlight function, noticing as she headed down the hall how it seemed to stretch farther than it did when the lights were on and kids were present.

She reached her classroom and saw it, too, was dark. Strange. She was supposed to be meeting her student Luke Thompson here. The text message he'd sent her earlier had indicated he was already at the school waiting. Had he given up waiting for her and left?

She reached up and flipped the light switch, but nothing happened. The room remained dark.

As she moved to open the blinds to at least give them some light, her foot caught on something on the floor and she stumbled, catching herself on one of the student desks. She turned the phone light to the floor to see what she'd tripped on and spotted something between the rows of desks. As she moved the light closer, she saw the outline of a hand…then an arm… then a body sprawled on the floor.

"Luke!" Claire knelt beside him, but he didn't move at the sound of his name. Her knees touched something wet and sticky. Dread filled her at the realization of what had happened.

She looked at her hand and saw blood. Luke's blood.

She stifled a scream. Panicking wouldn't do any good now. She needed to remain calm. If there was a chance Luke was still alive, she had to get help. She hit the keypad on her phone and tried to dial 9-1-1, but her hands were shaking so badly that she had to reenter the number.

Hang on, Luke!

She had just pressed Send on her call for help when someone grabbed her. Claire screamed and the phone slipped through her fingers and hit the floor with a crack. Her assailant clamped a heavy hand over her mouth and pinned her arms.

His breath was hot against her skin as he hissed into her ear. "You did this. You killed Luke with your meddling."

Terror gripped her at his words. Luke was dead. This man had killed him, and now he would kill her, too.

She struggled to break his hold, flailing her legs against a desk. It toppled over, taking the one beside it down, too. The wood and metal clanked against the tiled floor. She tried again to scream for help, but his heavy hand over her mouth prevented the sound from escaping. And who would hear her anyway in an empty school?

Oh, God, help me!

She was going to die right here in her classroom alongside one of her students.

Trixie. In his school.

DEA agent Matt Ross jiggled the handle on the southwest door by the cafeteria, and it opened just as Luke had assured him it would. He examined the lock and saw it didn't latch properly, preventing the locking mechanism from catching. He wondered how long it had been that way and how many Lakeshore High students had taken advantage of such a lack of security for skipping classes.

Luke had already assured him others knew about it. In fact, Lakeshore High had become a popular drug drop because of the failing security measures in the years since Matt had graduated.

He couldn't believe Trixie was in his old school. When he'd seen the report about a new and popular drug in his hometown of Lakeshore, Tennessee, he'd asked for the assignment to track down the suppliers. And Luke had been a wealth of information about the operation. The kid knew more than he should and was eager to share it with the DEA. The one thing he hadn't yet given Matt were names. Names of his supplier and the major players in the drug market in town. Matt hoped today he would finally get that information from Luke. The kid was scared. That was to be expected. Trixie might be a new drug, but it was already gaining popularity in the major cities and money was rolling in. Luke could find his very life in danger if anyone discovered he'd been talking with the DEA. Luke had chosen the school as a safe place to meet, sharing with Matt the information about the easy access through the southwest entrance.

Suddenly, a scream lit up the air.

Matt reached for his weapon, his entire body suddenly on alert. The school was supposed to be empty except for him and Luke, but that sounded like a woman's scream. He moved through the dark hallways, following the sounds of a struggle.

Everything went quiet…too quiet too suddenly. He peered cautiously into the classroom where he was sure the sounds had come from. A faint light on the floor revealed overturned desks. A struggle had definitely occurred here.

His gut clenched. Was he too late?

He moved slowly toward the light on the floor, now realizing it came from a dropped cell phone. Luke's? He spotted a shadow on the edge of the light and took a step closer, catching the outline of a body sprawled between the desks.

Luke.

He reached down and felt the boy's skin. It was cold. Luke was dead.

He raised his gun and scanned the room, his eyes already adjusting to the darkness. He'd trudged through darker environments during his time with the army rangers, but what he wouldn't give right now for a pair of night vision goggles. Someone was there in the darkness, though. He sensed their presence. Was the killer still on campus? Still in this room?

He pulled out his phone, clicked on the flashlight function and scanned the room again. He heard faint, muffled sounds coming from one corner of the room and he moved in that direction, his gun drawn and ready and his intuition on fire. The killer was still here.

"Let's just end this right now." Matt spoke through the darkness to the assailant, hoping for some sort of movement or change in breathing to pinpoint exactly where he was hiding.

He heard it again, that muffled grunt. It seemed to come from right in front of him. Suddenly, a figure in the darkness moved and someone was barreling toward him. He jumped back, then realized it was a woman being shoved at him. He reached out his arms and caught her, but the force of the assailant's push knocked him backward and he hit the floor. The lady fell on top of him, landing on his chest. He noted she was petite and light, and he caught the scent of berry shampoo as her long hair fluttered near his face. His cell phone clattered to the floor and the assailant ran out the door. Matt still had his gun in his hand, but he didn't dare fire into darkness.

The light from his phone illuminated Luke's face only inches away from them. The lady in his arms screamed and scrambled away, frightened.

"Are you okay?" Matt asked her. He reached for her arm and felt her quivering with fear. "Are you hurt?"

"I—I'm fine, but Luke…"

"I know." He leaped to his feet. "Stay here." He rushed out of the classroom and down the hall, his gun trained and ready, but when he saw the southwest door he'd closed standing open, he knew whoever had been here had fled.

He returned to the classroom and pulled open the window blinds, filling the room with sunlight.

He turned, surprised by the woman on the floor beside the body. He instantly recognized her petite frame, flowing dark hair and wide blue eyes as they stared up at him.

Claire Kendall. His former fiancée.

The love of his life.

The woman whose life he'd almost ended ten years ago.

In all the years she'd imagined bumping into Matt Ross again, Claire had never once imagined it would be over the body of one of her students. She stared up at him. He looked so different and yet so much like the Matt she remembered. He'd always been tall, but he seemed to have added a few inches since high school. The long arms and legs that had once been gangly were now solid and muscular and his chest and shoulders broad, a man instead of the boy she'd known ten years ago. His blond hair was cut shorter than she'd ever seen it, but she supposed it was longer now than it had been during his time in the army. His face was fuller, but his hazel eyes were still intense and his features sharp and handsome.

He knelt beside her. "Claire, what are you doing here? How do you know Luke Thompson?"

She was shocked that he knew Luke. "I'm a teacher at this school. This is my classroom. Luke is one of my students. How do you know him?" She recognized that troubled look on Matt's face and grew worried. "How do you know Luke?" she asked him again.

He helped her to her feet. "There's blood on your clothes."

She glanced down and saw dark stains smeared on her jeans and blouse. Her hands were also covered in blood. Luke's blood. "It's not mine."

"You're shaking." He took off his jacket and slipped it across her shoulders. "Let's get you out of here."

She went willingly with him, thankful for the support and for the jacket. She was trembling, although not from the cold. Shivers of fear and worry lit through her. She could still feel the clammy touch of that man's hand against her face and smell the rancid smell of his hot breath as he whispered to her. *You did this. You killed Luke with your meddling.*

What had he meant by that? All she'd done was try to help Luke. He'd wanted out of the drug business and she'd encouraged him. Had he heeded her advice and told his dealers that he didn't want to peddle their drugs anymore? Had they killed him because of it?

She stumbled as Matt led her toward the office. Her hip was stiff and sore after her ordeal, and she wished it didn't bother her so much. Other people might not even notice the residual slight limp, but Matt would notice. Matt was not just any other person. Thankfully, he said nothing as he led her to the office and Claire fell onto the couch, not certain her legs would carry her any farther. Matt walked out, then returned a moment later with a bottle of water. Her hands shook as she tried to lift it to her lips. Finally, he poured some into a paper cup and gave it to her.

The cool liquid felt soothing over her raw throat. She'd hardly been able to scream but still her throat was raw as if she had. She'd struggled against the force of that man's hand against her face, struggled for air to breathe. She didn't think he'd been trying to smother her, but his hand had essentially cut off her air supply.

Matt pulled up a chair and straddled it, his hazel eyes probing hers. "I need you to tell me exactly what happened."

"Shouldn't we call the police? I dialed 9-1-1 before that man grabbed me, but I don't know if the call went through."

"I am the police."

He pulled out his badge and she saw he now worked for the Drug Enforcement Administration. She knew he'd left the army, but she hadn't heard about this new position. Now his presence at the school made more sense. Luke was involved in drugs. Had Matt been here to arrest him?

"Tell me everything you remember. Why were you here at the school on a Sunday?"

Her hands shook as she outlined her morning, trying to remember every detail. "I received a text message from Luke an hour ago asking me to meet him at the school, so I came. The lights were out and even my classroom overhead light didn't work, but I had the flashlight on my phone. I found him lying on the floor. Before I could call for help, someone grabbed me."

"Did you see the man who grabbed you?"

"No. It was dark and he was behind me."

"Did you recognize his voice? Was there anything about him that was familiar?"

She shook her head. "It all happened so fast. He kept his hand over my mouth so I couldn't scream. I struggled, but I couldn't break free. When he heard you coming, he dragged me to the corner. The next thing I knew, he had shoved me toward you and we were on the floor."

"Did you let Luke into the building?"

"No. But everyone knows the door by the cafeteria doesn't latch well. He probably got in that way."

"Why did Luke ask to meet you today?"

His message hadn't said, but she'd hoped for some good news from him. "His message only said he had something important he needed to tell me."

"Were you aware he was selling drugs?"

"Yes. Luke came to me a few weeks ago and told me he'd been selling drugs, but that he wanted out. He gave his life to the Lord and didn't want to do it anymore, but he was afraid to tell his supplier. He said he was trying to find a safe way out of the business. When I saw his text, I thought he was going to tell me he'd finally done it."

"Did he ever tell you the name of his supplier or let something slip that could lead us to him?"

"No, he thought if I knew it would put me in danger." It seemed that had happened anyway. "I need to call his parents and tell them what happened."

"We'll have someone take care of that."

She looked at him. "He was a good kid. He was trying to get his life together."

She heard the sound of sirens growing closer. Matt stood and peeked out the window. "I guess the police did receive your call."

A moment later, the doors opened and the school was flooded with uniformed police officers.

She spotted her friend Preston, a detective with the Lakeshore Police Department, directing several of the officers to secure the school. When he spotted her through the window separating the office from the foyer, his face paled and he rushed to her.

"Claire! We received an emergency call from this location. What are you doing here?" He grabbed her and pulled her into a hug.

"Preston, it's Luke Thompson. He's dead."

"The kid you've been ministering to? What happened?"

"He sent me a text message asking me to meet him, but when I arrived, he was on the floor and someone else was in the room. He grabbed me. If Matt hadn't arrived when he did…" She turned to look at him, suddenly realizing she owed her life to Matt. She also realized she hadn't introduced the two men. "Matt, this is my friend Detective Preston Ware. He's with the Lakeshore PD. Preston, this is Matt Ross. He's with the DEA."

Preston's look of surprise was obvious. "Matt Ross? As in…"

She knew exactly what he was referring to. Preston was aware of her history with Matt.

Matt responded with a chagrined look. "Yes, that Matt Ross." He held out his hand to shake Preston's. "Nice to meet you."

Preston reluctantly took the hand he offered.

"Whoever grabbed Claire got away before I could stop him. The body is in Claire's classroom. It's the fourth—"

"I know where her classroom is." Preston turned back to Claire. "Stay here. I'll need to ask you some questions after I see the crime scene."

She nodded, expecting it would be the same questions Matt had asked her. And she would have the same answers she'd given him. She didn't know who'd killed Luke and she hadn't seen her attacker's face.

"I've already secured the scene," Matt assured him.

Preston shot him a cautious smile. "You don't mind if we double-check that, do you?"

She sensed a simmering dislike between the two men. It was more than their cautious smiles and easy-going manners. Beneath the surface, there seemed to be a palpable desire in both of them to strike out against the other. Matt's folded arms as he informed Preston about the details of the case. Preston's defensive stance.

She was glad when they both walked out. She wasn't surprised that Preston was leery of Matt. After all, she'd cried on his shoulder numerous times through the years about her ordeal.

But what possible reason could Matt have against Preston?

He didn't like it. Nope, he didn't like it one bit.

Who was this guy who'd claimed Claire as his own with one call of her name?

A feeling of satisfaction had washed over him as he reached out to shake Preston's hand. Claire had called him a friend and everyone knew what that meant—platonic, non-boyfriend friend. And Preston's grip as they shook was firmer than it needed to be, an obvious acknowledgment of territory. His stance was clear—back off! Apparently, he hadn't caught on to Claire's reference to him as her "friend." He was still clinging hopelessly to the delusion that they could one day be more.

It wouldn't happen. If Matt knew one thing about Claire, it was that she believed love should be passionate and overwhelming...the way they'd once been. If there was no passion, in her mind, there was no romance.

"Claire said you were DEA. May I ask what you were doing here? Is the DEA performing an investigation we need to know about?"

"Luke was a DEA informant. We were hoping he could give us information that would break up a drug ring working out of the school."

"What kind of drug ring?"

"It's a new drug called Trixie. It's a stimulant that—"

"I know it. High-priced. Very dangerous."

"And popular with the kids. Our intel says there's a major business working out of Lakeshore High. We were just starting our investigation." They stepped into the classroom and Matt saw Luke on the floor, his throat slit and blood everywhere. His gut clenched. Luke had been his key to unlocking the drug ring operating in his hometown. Now, instead of an informant, he was a murder victim.

And Claire had somehow stumbled into the middle of his investigation and onto the radar of a killer.

"You shouldn't be in here."

"Relax," Matt said. "This isn't my first crime scene. I know how to be careful."

"I don't care how many crime scenes you say you've

been to, this one is mine and I say you need to leave. This isn't a DEA investigation anymore. This is a murder, and homicide is my jurisdiction."

Matt turned to look at him, the territorial protective vibe going again. This was *his* investigation. Claire was *his* friend. It was all about *him*, wasn't it? "Luke was a DEA informant, and I'm still investigating a drug ring operating out of this school. I would like to be kept involved." He could tell the detective wasn't happy about his role and he wasn't surprised, but he was also sure it had less to do with him being DEA than with him being Claire's ex.

"Look, I'm not just some guy off the street. I'm an old friend of Claire's and I don't want to see anything happen to her."

"Oh, I know exactly who you are," Preston countered, turning to stare right into Matt's face. "You're the scumbag who wrapped his car around a telephone pole on prom night, then left Claire battered and brokenhearted while you took off to join the army."

Matt shouldered his tirade. It wasn't exactly correct. He hadn't left Claire in the car. It had been weeks later that he'd left town when his prayers to God for her recovery went unanswered. He hadn't been on speaking terms with the Almighty since. But Preston got the gist of the story correct, and who was Matt to squabble over details. He'd caused the wreck, then had left her when his guilt got too heavy to bear.

But that didn't change today's situation. Claire was in danger, and he wasn't stepping aside this time.

"That was a long time ago."

"That's right, it was. Your connection to Claire

ended the moment you walked out on her." Preston turned and knelt to examine the body.

Enough talk. Matt got serious. "You are aware that Luke was dead long before he supposedly sent Claire that text message?"

"We haven't even determined time of death yet."

"I've seen my share of bodies. That boy has been dead at least four hours. Claire said she received the text an hour ago. Someone wanted her to come here, possibly just to find Luke, but maybe for more than that. Her life is in danger, and if you think I'm going to leave until I know she's safe, then you don't know me as well as you think you do."

Matt walked out, leaving him to process the crime scene. He focused on trying to calm down, but it was a daunting task given the surge of adrenaline that had pulsed through his veins from the moment he'd heard that first scream, and reinforced from the realization that the woman on top of him had once been the love of his life. It had taken all his strength to pull away from her and lead her to a chair in the school's office, but his instincts had kicked in, reminding him that his priority had to be preserving the scene and that meant getting Claire out of the area as soon as possible.

Preston's men would go over every detail of that room and the body, but Matt didn't need an autopsy report to tell him what he already knew.

The killer had lured Claire into that classroom.

It didn't take long from the time the police arrived for a crowd to form outside the school. Onlookers appeared along with the television news teams.

Claire peeked out the window and saw the three

local news channels all setting up in front of the school. She noticed many of the students and the worry on their faces. When she turned on the television in the office, the news channels were reporting a body was found at the high school, but they had not identified it as a student.

What would happen to those kids when they learned one of their own was dead? When they heard it was Luke Thompson who'd been killed? They would be devastated.

You killed Luke with your meddling.

Those words rushed back to her and she shuddered. She'd only wanted to help Luke, not get him killed.

Chills ran up her spine. She might have been lying beside Luke if Matt hadn't arrived. But what was he doing at the school? She wasn't surprised to see him in town, since she knew his sister, Alisa, was getting married in two weeks and most of the family was returning for the wedding. But what had he been doing at the school on a Sunday afternoon?

She realized those were the same questions he'd asked of her. Only, she'd told him why she was there. He had yet to explain his presence. She'd been so thankful he was there that she hadn't even thought to question him about why he'd come.

The roar of the crowd outside grew louder as the front door to the school pushed open and she saw Principal Spencer enter. He let the door close behind him as he headed into the office.

"Claire. What are you doing here? The news is saying a body was found on campus?"

"It was one of our students, Luke Thompson."

"Luke? What do they think happened?"

"Someone killed him. I found his body and some-one was there. He tried to grab me."

Principal Spencer's face was instantly full of con-cern for her. "Are you hurt? How did you get away?"

"Someone else rescued me. I don't know what would have happened if he hadn't arrived when he did."

"Has anyone notified Luke's parents? They'll be devastated."

"I don't know."

"I'll go find out. Will you start calling the faculty and let them know what's happened? We'll need to coordinate a response, arrange for counselors and such."

"Certainly."

She hadn't thought about calling anyone, not even him. She supposed that was why he was the princi-pal. He had a take-charge attitude and remained calm during a time of crisis.

She found a phone list on the secretary's desk and began making calls.

Matt returned to the classroom and stared at the body on the floor. He couldn't help thinking what a shame it was that someone so young was gone. Yes, he'd seen death before—too many times before—but it still struck him as tragic. This kid was only seven-teen at best, much too young to have been caught up in drugs and drug rings. But it was an all too com-mon tale, he'd discovered since coming to work for the DEA. Kids and drugs. Devastated lives. Shattered families. He was tired of the senselessness of it all.

Preston stood over the body, examining it. "It looks like his throat was slit. We'll have to wait for an autopsy report, but I suspect that will be the cause of death."

Matt had to concur. He, too, suspected Luke's throat was cut, but an autopsy would tell them how quickly he died. Was this the work of an experienced killer or an amateur? The answer to that question would provide them leads in finding the person responsible.

Preston stood. "We haven't located the murder weapon yet, but I'll have my guys conduct a search."

"We should start along the path he took when he ran out. It's possible he tossed the weapon when he ran."

Preston nodded. "That could include the parking lot and the woods behind the school." He stared out the window at the crowd already gathered. "And the area has already been contaminated. I'll have someone clear out this crowd." Preston got on the radio and issued his instructions for the search.

A uniformed officer poked his head through the door and addressed Preston. "The school principal is here. He'd like to speak with someone."

Preston nodded. "Tell him I'll be right out."

Matt followed Preston into the hallway. A tall, sandy-haired man was waiting for them. He extended his hand. "I'm Bill Spencer, principal of Lakeshore High School. Can you tell me what happened?"

Preston took the lead. "Only that the body of one of your students was discovered in this classroom. We suspect foul play."

"Claire said it was Luke Thompson. Was anyone

else involved? Do you have any idea why this happened?"

"We're still investigating, Principal Spencer."

"Of course. Well, you can see half the town is already aware a body has been found. I'd like to be able to tell my students and teachers something about what happened here."

"We just don't have enough evidence yet to draw conclusions, much less make them public."

"Will we be able to open the school for classes tomorrow?"

"We're still processing the scene. It's too early to tell."

"I understand, but it's imperative we get these kids back into school as soon as possible. It's an important element to helping them cope. We'll be calling in mental health counselors to assist the students in their grieving process."

Matt was surprised when Preston seemed to offer the principal something. Protecting the crime scene should have been the most important thing. "For right now, this entire hall and portions of the parking lot and back forty are off-limits. We may open those to students if we don't find anything, but this classroom will be inaccessible until we finish our investigation. It's a crime scene. But I think you'll be able to reopen for classes by Tuesday."

Principal Spencer nodded. "We'll utilize the cafeteria, auditorium and the courtyard for the overflow. I'll make an announcement about the school reopening Tuesday. And don't worry, Detective, we will keep this area off-limits. We won't do anything to compromise this investigation. This tragedy will shake the school to its foundations. Luke was well liked. We'll be concentrating on helping the students cope with his death. I've already got Claire placing calls to the other teachers."

"The parents are here," a uniformed officer told them.

"Would you mind if I'm there when you talk to the Thompsons about Luke?" the principal asked. "I think it would help for them to see a familiar face."

"We'll have to ask some difficult questions of the family," Preston told him. "Perhaps it would be better if you were there. This is Agent Ross of the DEA. He'll be joining us, as well. We'll need to use your office."

"Certainly," Principal Spencer said. "Anything I can do to help."

Luke's parents were ushered into the principal's office. They'd already been informed that their son was dead. Mrs. Thompson sat quietly, shock pressing on her heavily made-up face. Her mascara hadn't even run and Matt had to wonder if she'd shed a tear yet. Shock had that effect on some people. It would hit her, though, and it would be hard and painful. Mr. Thompson expressed his grief differently—he was vocal.

"I want to know what my son was doing here," he demanded. "And why was that teacher meeting him here alone? I want answers."

"We're working on that, Mr. Thompson." Preston was the picture of grace and ease, and Matt had to admit he admired the man's ability to handle this difficult situation. "We all want answers. When was the last time you saw Luke?"

His mother's hands shook, so she clenched them

together, fighting to keep her composure. "Last night. He said he was going out with friends."

"You didn't see him when he came home?"

"No, I was already asleep. Luke was a very independent boy. He didn't take a lot of oversight. If he said he was going to be home by midnight, he was. I didn't think anything about it. I left the house early this morning for a meeting. I assumed he was still sleeping upstairs."

"Luke was a good kid," Mr. Thompson said. "He had a lot of friends."

"Do you know if Luke was involved in any kind of drug use?"

"What? No. I would know if my son was doing drugs. Luke was too smart to do something that dumb."

Matt stepped forward and produced his DEA credentials. "My name is Matt Ross. I'm with the DEA. Your son contacted me with information he had about a drug ring operating in Lakeshore. I believe that's what got him killed."

"You think Luke was using drugs?" Mr. Thompson asked.

"We believe he was doing more than taking them. We believe he was selling, as well," Matt said.

Matt watched his reaction and saw the typical parental denial. It seemed genuine, though. It didn't appear that the Thompsons knew about Luke's extracurricular activities.

"We gave Luke everything he needed," Mr. Thompson said. "Why would he be involved with selling drugs? He certainly didn't need the money. I don't want you spreading these lies about my son. He wasn't doing drugs and he certainly wasn't selling them, regardless of what you say. Someone killed my son. Concentrate on finding that person, not on vilifying my boy."

It wasn't the first time Matt had seen parents refuse to admit the truth about their kids. Luke was dead and they would do whatever they could to preserve their memory of him. But Matt had another job— uncovering the truth. And the truth was that Luke had reached out to him, offering information about a drug ring operating out of the school. The kid had known something. If only they'd had the opportunity to talk more in depth.

His mind skimmed over the initial details Luke had given on the phone. He'd identified the drug being sold in his school as Trixie, and he'd hinted someone inside was involved.

Had Luke told Claire who it was? Was she too frightened to tell, after seeing what had happened to Luke? Or was she truly as innocent as she claimed to be?

Someone believed she knew more, or else why lure her to the school? To find out what Luke had told her? Or to make certain she didn't know more than she should? If he knew the answer to that, he might know whether the attacker had planned to question her or kill her if Matt hadn't shown up.

How had Claire gotten involved in this mess? The Claire he'd known had been kind and innocent. It didn't matter that years had passed since he'd last seen her. He couldn't imagine she'd changed. People simply didn't change that much. But then when he'd known her, she hadn't been counseling drug dealers, either. Had her involvement with Luke placed a target on her back?

Matt remained quiet as Preston ended the conference with the Thompsons, assuring them again that the police would do everything in their power to bring Luke's killer to justice. As they were leaving, Matt slipped out. He walked back to the main office, but Claire wasn't there. He found her in one of the other classrooms using the sink in the corner to fill a coffeepot with water. She still wore his jacket, which made her look small and petite. Wisps of dark hair fell across her cheek, loosened from their clip during her struggle. They framed her beautiful face and her big blue eyes—eyes he'd spent years gazing lovingly into, and many more years dreaming of.

She eyed him watching her. "I figure they'll be wanting some coffee soon. I thought I would make a pot."

He smiled. That was so Claire. Trying to take care of everyone else when she was the one who'd experienced an awful fright. He was suddenly tongue-tied, uncertain of what to say to her in this moment when there was nothing but the past between them.

"How have you been?" she asked, starting the awful, awkward conversation he'd known was coming.

"I've been good," he told her. "Real good." He rubbed his face, trying without success to wipe away the overwhelming desire to take her in his arms again and assure her that everything would be fine. But as Preston Ware had pointed out, that was no longer his right to do. "So you became a teacher? What do you teach?"

"Chemistry."

"You always were good at science. Better than me, that's for sure." He glanced around at the room they were in. He'd been holding back a slew of memories that had emerged the moment he'd stepped through the door into Lakeshore High. He'd spent four years at this school, good years. "Didn't we have a class in this room?"

She nodded. "Western Civ."

He grinned, remembering those days. "Coach Rollins. I wonder whatever happened to him."

"He died of a heart attack last year."

He forgot he wasn't just reminiscing with some old friend. She'd been here in town. She'd kept up with all those people he'd left behind. "I'm sorry to hear that."

"Look, Matt, there are a lot of places in this building, even in this town, where we took classes or hung out together. I know it must be awkward for you, but I face those places every day. I put those memories behind me a long time ago."

Ouch, right to the point. "Claire, I owe you an apology."

"Don't. Please don't apologize. We were just kids back then."

"The accident—"

"Was just an accident, Matt."

"I shouldn't have been drinking and driving."

"We were both drinking that night. We both used bad judgment."

"Then you at least have to let me apologize for leaving the way I did."

"It's not necessary."

He flashed back to the night of the accident and the sight of her broken body being pulled out from the wrecked car. It was the image of her he'd carried with him for the past ten years. "You look good, Claire. Are you... Is everything okay?"

She nodded. "It took a few surgeries and a lot of rehab, but I'm okay now." She rubbed her hip unconsciously and he wondered if it bothered her. He'd noticed her limping earlier. "You are hurt," he said, motioning to her hip.

She reddened, then waved away his concern. "It's nothing."

"You need to have that checked out."

"It's nothing," she insisted, and the red on her face deepened. "It's from an old injury. It just acts up on occasion."

He realized her old injury was from the car wreck and shame filled him. She was still suffering from his wrong choices even after all these years.

She set the coffeepot to the side. "Actually, I'm tired. It's been a very long day and I'm ready to go home and crawl into bed."

"That's a bad idea," Matt said. "You shouldn't be alone until we find the person who killed Luke and attacked you."

"I'll be fine. I was just in the wrong place at the wrong time. No one is after me."

"We don't know that, Claire. You could still be in danger."

She glanced up at him, curiosity pooling in her eyes. "Why? What did you find?"

"Luke didn't send you that text asking you to come to the school. He couldn't have. He was already dead by the time that text was sent."

"But it came from his phone. How can you possibly know that with any certainty?"

"I saw enough dead bodies during my time with the rangers and I'm telling you Luke has been dead for hours, which means someone else used his phone to send you that text message. Whoever it was lured you here and was waiting for you, Claire."

He saw her mind racing. "Who would do that? Who would want to hurt me?"

"That's a good question, and one we need to figure out."

"I'm sure the text thing was just a fluke. Sometimes text messages get hung up in cyberspace."

He shook his head. He'd meant it when he'd said he wasn't leaving until he knew Claire was safe…and that was looking less and less likely. There was no way he was going to let her go home alone. She would be a sitting target. "Why don't you go and stay with your folks for a few days? Just until we have time to sort all of this out?"

"My parents are on a cruise."

"What about friends? I would feel better if you weren't alone."

"Matt, I appreciate your concern, but I'm fine. I'm sure you're worried about nothing. Like you said, I don't know anything, so there's no reason to believe my life is in danger."

Her stubborn streak hadn't changed, and past experience told him that once she'd made up her mind, it was no use arguing. All he could do was try to figure out who killed Luke as quickly as possible. "Fine, but I'm driving you home."

"That's not necessary. I have my car."

"I know, but I would feel better if you'd let me drive you." Drive her home. Make sure she's safely inside. Then back to his life and let Detective Preston Ware step into the role of good guy. It no longer fit him.

She chewed on her bottom lip, a clear indication she was nervous about being alone with him. At least that hadn't changed. Finally, she gave a resigned sigh and agreed to let him drive her.

What on earth had she been thinking?

Allowing Matt to drive her home had been a phenomenal mistake.

She nearly burst out laughing as he climbed into her Volkswagen Bug, his long legs claiming the front seat and his knees nearly in his chest. He pushed back the seat to its farthest position, then started the engine.

"Are you sure you want to do this?" she asked him. "How will you get back to your vehicle?"

"It's only a couple of miles back to the school. I've hiked farther than that with a loaded pack in the pouring down rain. A clear spring night with a slight breeze will make it a piece of cake."

She'd imagined him before doing his army training, and now she had an image of him carrying a heavy pack in the rain.

One more image of Matt Ross to file away.

He looked so different and yet so much like the Matt she remembered. He was taller and broader, a man instead of the boy she'd known. But his hazel eyes were still intense and his gaze on her still held the power to make her toes tingle. She turned to stare out the window as she felt her face flush with embarrassment.

She pointed the way and he turned into her driveway and stopped the car. He got out and walked her to her door.

"Thank you for bringing me home, Matt."

"You're welcome. It's the least I could do for you, Claire."

She shuddered as he placed his hand on her arm and walked with her toward the door. The air was chilly, but it wasn't as much from the cold that she shivered. This reminded her that she was wearing his jacket.

"I should give this back now," she said, slipping out of his coat and handing it to him. "It was good to see you again, Matt." She didn't think she could stand another ending with Matt Ross, but at least this time she could have a goodbye.

She turned to say it and spotted a car slowing down as it approached her house.

"Claire, get down!" Matt shouted, grabbing her and throwing her to the ground as a slew of gunfire lit up the night and rained down on her house.

The car roared away, tires screeching, and the gunfire stopped. Fear ripped through her as she realized the gunfire was aimed at her.

Someone was really trying to kill her!

"Claire, are you okay? Are you hurt?"

She shook her head, unable to find her voice. Two violent attempts in one day. She wasn't sure she was made for this type of action.

Matt reached for her face and turned it so he could look at her. His eyes were ablaze with anger and fear and she could feel his heart racing even with the distance between them.

And suddenly the dam broke inside of her. This was just too much for her to take. The death of a student, a drive-by shooting and Matt Ross returning to her life all in one day? She fell into his arms, not even caring what he must think of her. She was afraid, and she was thankful Matt was here to protect her.

TWO

"This will sting," the EMT said as he treated the wound where a bullet had grazed Matt's shoulder.

He barely flinched as the EMT fixed him up. It wasn't serious. He'd had serious wounds before, but this episode tonight had shaken him and he didn't have to wonder why. Claire was huddled in the cab of a police car, head down and shaking with fear.

He couldn't believe he'd been prepared to leave her at the house alone. What if he had? What if he hadn't been there when the shots came? Anger and bitterness surged through him. He would find whoever was doing this and he would make them pay.

He'd had one mission in coming home—to fly under the radar and get out of town with information about a dangerous drug ring. That mission had failed big-time. Now he had a new one—to keep Claire safe.

He headed for the car and knelt beside her.

"How's your arm?" she asked.

"I'm fine. I've had worse injuries shaving in the mornings."

She smiled at his attempt to lighten the mood. "The police want to know what I saw. The problem is I don't know what I saw. I remember a car slowing down, but I can't remember the details. They want make, model, color."

He'd been trained to notice such things and he'd already given the local police a description as well as the tag number, although he doubted it would result in anything. The car was more than likely stolen or the plates had been changed. He doubted they would have an easy time locating the car.

"You can't stay here," he told her. "It's not safe for you to be alone until we figure this out."

She nodded, obviously realizing he'd been right. "I can't go to a friend's house. I won't put anyone in danger because of me. I'll get a hotel room."

He wouldn't argue with her over that. He had a hotel reservation, and getting Claire an adjoining room and having her close by would make him feel better. It wasn't perfect, but it would do.

Matt loaded Claire's bags into the trunk of his rental car, which he'd retrieved from the school parking lot while she was being questioned by the police. Her Bug was bullet-riddled and inoperable, but that didn't matter because he'd already determined that she wasn't going anywhere without him. Not until he knew she was safe, and that meant finding out who was behind the drug ring.

He drove to the hotel he'd booked and asked for adjoining rooms, making sure they had good sight lines to the parking lot in case someone decided to attack them at the hotel.

Claire unpacked, then stood at the door and watched Matt as he unloaded his computer equipment and set up a mini office on the desk.

"I'm sorry to take you away from your family. You come to town to see them and now you're stuck here protecting me."

He focused his attention on setting up his computer, hoping his expression wouldn't give him away. Once upon a time, she'd been able to read him like an open book and know when he was holding something back. He wondered if she still could.

She stared at him, then folded her arms in a determined stance he recognized. She glanced at his suitcase, noting the few folded pieces of clothing. His phone was on the nightstand and she must have realized he hadn't used it once to phone his parents. "They don't know you're in town, do they?"

"I didn't come to Lakeshore for a family reunion, Claire. I came to follow up on a lead about a drug ring operating in town."

"But how could you come back to Lakeshore and not call your family? You had a hotel reservation. You weren't planning on seeing them, were you?"

"No, no, I wasn't."

"But I thought everyone was in town for Alisa's wedding."

"That's not until the weekend after next."

She watched him for several moments and it seemed she was looking right into his soul. Could she see the years of pain and grief behind the green of his eye? Ten years had taken a toll on him yet she still looked as sweet and beautiful as she had in high school.

He saw a tinge of sympathy in her eyes...then she reached for her hip and bit back pain and her sympathy for him seemed to falter. She walked in and sat down. "Why are you here, Matt? I mean, why Luke? How did you get involved in this?"

He was glad to see she was still direct and to the point. "We've been tracking shipments of synthesized drug chemicals throughout the Southeast. The ring we've been tracking has a special chemical signature. They ship to suppliers throughout the region who then mix and package the chemicals into a salable drug. Luke's information confirmed for us that they were recruiting kids to help sell in schools."

"I knew he wanted out of the drug business, but I had no idea he was in contact with the DEA. How did that happen?"

"I never had the opportunity to fully question him, but he apparently contacted the FBI first. They didn't have jurisdiction, so they referred him to the DEA, where he spoke a couple of times to one of our intelligence agents. He's the one who contacted me. I tried several times to get information out of Luke, but he was too afraid to speak more on the phone. He wanted a face-to-face meeting, so we set up the meeting at the school. I was hoping to learn the identity of Luke's supplier. From there, we could have worked our way up the ladder and possibly taken out those behind this ring. Luke's information was the first real break we've had. The DEA has been trying to infiltrate this ring for several years without success. Losing Luke will be a big hit to taking them down."

"That's it? A kid is dead and all you can think about is the loss to your investigation?" She looked disgusted by his attitude, but she didn't understand the scope of what was happening.

"Kids are dying every day, Claire. This drug, Trixie,

it's deadly. So far, we've counted fourteen deaths re-lated to it. One was a thirteen-year-old. These drug dealers know it's dangerous and yet they're still push-ing it to kids. I am sorry Luke is dead, but I have to keep my focus on the bigger picture. He never got a chance to share information with me that could have toppled this ring, but maybe finding the person who killed him can do it instead." She hung her head and he could tell she was wiped out. Ten years may have taken its toll on him, but the day had taken its toll on her. "Why don't you get some sleep? You must be tired."

"I'm not sure I'll be able to sleep. So much has happened today." She shuddered and Matt walked to her and rubbed her arms, noting the goose bumps.

"You don't have to worry. You're safe here, Claire. I'm right next door and I won't let anything happen to you."

She nodded. "Good night." She went back into her room and closed the door between them, leaving it cracked slightly as he'd requested.

Matt was too keyed up to sleep. He wouldn't rest easy until he knew Claire was safe. He should have made other arrangements when Luke wanted to meet at the school. But how was he to know that Luke even knew Claire? He'd had no idea she was teaching at Lakeshore. In truth, he'd had no idea what she was doing at all. He'd made a point not to know. The less he'd known about her, the easier it had been for him to go on.

But she looked good, better than he'd expected, since he hadn't seen her since the night of the wreck.

He got out of bed and opened his laptop, typing up an official report of the day's events, including the murder of his informant and his intention to follow up on the murder investigation in the hopes the killer would lead him to Luke's supplier, and emailing it to his supervisor at the DEA. He'd phoned him earlier while he was at the school to update him, but the official report was needed for the file.

One thing he liked about his DEA job was the autonomy he had. He didn't have someone always looking over his shoulder or second-guessing his decisions. He had the leeway to extend his stay in Lakeshore to follow up on the murder investigation…and to keep Claire safe in the meantime.

She'd stepped on a land mine without even realizing it. He was sure the shooting at her house was meant to be a warning to her to keep her mouth shut. Whoever had killed Luke had obviously wanted to know what information the boy had shared with her and that made her a target.

He paced the floor, anger biting into him. One more person he cared about was in danger. He didn't think he could stand it if something happened to her. He'd lost too many people he cared about in the ambush that took out most of his ranger team. He didn't think he could stand losing anyone else.

Claire changed into her pajamas, then crawled into bed and pulled the covers high over her like a protective shield against the fear that threatened to overwhelm her.

Matt's presence in the next room was comforting, and she heard him moving around until finally the light from beneath the door went out. She closed her eyes, but as she'd expected, sleep evaded her.

Her brain was a scramble of today's events, from Luke's murder to the drive-by shooting to the sudden reappearance of Matt Ross in her life.

Matt was a trained ranger with the skills to protect her. She'd been studying through the Old Testament recently in her quiet time with God and now the parallels of one story and her current situation came into focus. Like Joseph, Matt had been taken from those he cared about in order to prepare him for something greater, something that would ultimately protect her. God had previously prepared him for this task, and for that Claire was thankful. God was on her side. With the assurance that God had sent her a protector, Claire slipped peacefully into sleep.

The regular Monday morning staff meeting today would be a somber affair given the events of yesterday. The death of a student was a rare but tragic event, and Claire knew this morning the teachers would be formulating a plan for dealing with the aftermath, including arranging counseling for the students who needed it.

She arrived for the meeting and several faculty members asked about her. The news of her involvement had already spread, but she wondered how many of these teachers also knew about Luke's drug connections or the involvement of Matt and the DEA. They'd soon find out, since Matt had accompanied her this morning and was preparing to speak to the group.

Principal Spencer took control of the staff meeting. "The district superintendent has called in special crisis counselors. They'll be arriving today to meet with any of the staff and faculty who would like to speak with them. They'll also be conducting training today about helping the students cope with the tragedy that's occurred here. When the students return tomorrow, it'll be our jobs to let them know that counselors are there for them to speak with if they need it. We'll be congregating mostly in the auditorium and cafeteria today, but I have gotten word from LPD that we'll be able to reopen the back hall for classes tomorrow."

After outlining what would be a long and emotionally difficult day, he introduced Matt.

"This is Agent Matt Ross from the DEA. He's going to be here helping us update our security measures while working with the police to investigate Luke's death. He'll be setting up in the security office, but you may see him roaming around the halls and asking questions. Please provide him any information you believe might be helpful. As always, the safety of our students is a top priority at Lakeshore High School."

Matt stepped forward and addressed the group. "I didn't know Luke Thompson well. I'd only spoken to him twice, but I know how his death has shattered this school and this community. But Luke alerted me and the DEA to a serious problem occurring here at Lakeshore. A dangerous drug called Trixie has been moving through this community and this school. I can't confirm or deny whether Luke's death had anything to do with this drug ring because that investigation is still ongoing, but I intend to find out how these drugs are getting into the hands of these kids. I grew up in Lakeshore. I went to this high school and my family still lives here. This is my home. I know that each of you are here because you, too, care about these students. Together, we can put an end to this ring that's preying on our kids."

Claire saw his passion and was happy to hear him proclaim this was his home after he'd confessed to her that he hadn't even phoned his folks yet. She glanced around her and wondered how many of her fellow teachers knew their history and knew that Matt had fled Lakeshore over ten years ago. Whatever reasons he'd had for staying away for so long, he'd pushed them aside in order to get the job done.

Matt finished addressing the faculty and Principal Spencer ended the meeting and dismissed them. He called Claire to stay. "Your classroom is still a crime scene and I've been told we can't go in there, so we'll relocate your classes to the science lab for the time being."

She wasn't sure she wanted to return to that classroom, but she knew she would. Life had to go on. But Lakeshore had a new state-of-the-art lab that all the science classes shared. It would mean rearranging schedules so the other classes could still have lab time, but they could make it work for a while. "That will be fine."

Principal Spencer gazed at her knowingly and placed a comforting hand on her shoulder. "You've been through an ordeal. Are you sure you're up to being here?"

"I want to be here. I need to get my classroom set up. The students will need some kind of normalcy when they return tomorrow."

He walked over and closed the door, giving them

privacy. "I have to ask this question, Claire. Why were you here?"

"Luke sent me a text asking me to meet him here… or at least I thought it was Luke."

"And you came? I don't understand why you would meet a student at an empty school on the weekend."

"I've been ministering to Luke for several weeks. When I got the text, I thought maybe he'd had a breakthrough."

"And what about the drugs? Did you know he was involved in selling drugs at the school?"

"I did know. He told me he wanted out, but he was frightened his supplier wouldn't let him go."

"Did he tell you who his supplier was?"

"I don't know anything about Luke's drug supplier. I was just trying to help Luke."

"You can imagine my shock to learn one of our own students was supplying a highly dangerous drug throughout the school. As a teacher and a faculty member, you should have let someone know when you discovered this."

"I didn't want to get him expelled or arrested. He wanted to turn his life around. He wanted out. He promised me he wasn't selling them anymore."

"Still, I wish you had come to me. Maybe if you had, things would have turned out differently."

You killed Luke with your meddling. Those haunting words replayed in her mind no matter how often she tried to push them away. She remembered the hot breath on her neck and the bite in his threatening tone. Tears stung her eyes, but she pushed them back. She'd only wanted to help Luke, not get him killed. "I need to get my classroom set up for tomorrow."

The principal nodded, and his face was sympathetic. "I hope you know you can come to me, Claire. Anytime you need to talk, I'm available."

"Thank you," she said, then walked out.

Matt was leaning against the wall in the hallway, waiting for her. His arms were folded and he gave her a lazy grin that reminded her of all the times in school that she'd seen him waiting for her. Everything about having him here seemed to remind her of the past.

"What did he have to say?"

"Same as everyone else. Am I okay? Should I be here? Do I know anything about Luke's drug supplier?"

"And what did you tell him?"

"I told him just what I told you, Matt. I'm fine, I need to be here for my students and Luke never shared that information with me. I have no idea who Luke was working for. I wish I did. I wish I had demanded to know. Then I would know who to blame for all of this."

She felt her voice quiver as she spoke and she was nearing hysterics. It had already been a difficult morning and it was still early. How would she ever make it through the day?

Matt reached out and hugged her in a comforting manner. "We'll figure it out. We'll find out who is behind this drug ring and who killed Luke. I won't let his death be in vain. I won't let them win. That's a promise, Claire."

She felt calmer with her face pressed against his chest, but she knew she shouldn't. He'd broken more than her heart when he'd left her. He'd shattered her life. She couldn't forgive that and she could never forget. She pushed away from him and stared up into his

hazel eyes, seeing determination and that hardheaded
stubbornness she remembered so well, and she believed him. He could keep her safe and he could find
out who was preying on these kids.

While Claire joined the other faculty members in
workshops given by trained counselors on ways to
help bereaved students, Matt worked with the school's
three security guards on staff to secure the campus
for the returning students. He recognized right away
that they'd been undertrained for the job they'd been
given, but he armed them with directives for simple
security measures such as making sure all the outside
doors locked properly and that they were regularly
patrolling the hallways. Such measures would make
trafficking drugs into the school more difficult, but it
might also help draw out Luke's supplier, who would
be hustling to make different arrangements now that
Luke was dead and the police and DEA were investigating. Common sense should have told the supplier
now was the time to put a hold on business, but Matt
knew from experience that arrogance combined with
greed rarely had anyone using common sense.

He set himself up in the security office and thumbed
through reports the local police had delivered to him
about interviews from the day before. He'd left the grunt
work to the locals, asking only that he be alerted if they
uncovered any relevant information during their interviews. Preston had sent over a stack of flagged files,
but as Matt scoured through them he could find few
reasons that would account for them being flagged. He
wondered if this was another of Preston's ways of as-
serting his dominance over Matt or if the local police

were just worried about having the DEA peering over their shoulders as they investigated.

He set those files aside and opened the one with the crime scene photos, hoping they would provide more answers than he'd seen at the scene. Initial toxicology reports confirmed no drugs in Luke's system, which strengthened Claire's claim that the kid was no longer using. But so many questions still remained unanswered.

Cold chills seeped through him as he realized he might just have easily been looking at images of Claire dead beside Luke. He dropped the photo he held. He didn't usually let his emotions get the better of him, but at the thought of her being killed, a black ball of dread filled him. Had he not arrived at the school, she could have been. Had he not been with her at the house, she might have been killed.

He wasn't a praying man, not anymore, not for a long time, but he was thankful anyway. Thankful that he'd found his way back to Lakeshore just in the nick of time.

After the counseling workshop, Claire concentrated on setting up her new classroom in the science lab. Because it was a newer addition to the school, the lab was on the other side of campus from the science hall, but it was a fully updated, well-equipped lab mostly funded by parent donations. This district was home to many prominent medical professionals who insisted on a top-notch science program at the high school with the aim of making certain their offspring were well prepared for college science curriculums.

In fact, nearly half of the last graduating class had gone on to major in premed in college.

She raided the supply closet, loading a box with paper, pens and whiteboard markers as well as various other supplies she might need, then hurried across campus. She wanted to have her new classroom area ready before the students returned tomorrow.

When her desk was fully set up, she turned her attention to prepping lab experiments. She had ordered three one-pound packages of sodium metal. She took them out and began cutting them up into smaller pieces.

Matt arrived at her door and smiled at her in that lazy, way-too-attractive manner he had. "Busy?"

Her pulse quickened as he walked in and she struggled to keep her voice level as she answered. "Just prepping for an experiment."

He glanced around at the lab. "I seem to recall we first met in chemistry class."

"Yes, my family had just moved to town and I walked into class and you were the only one who didn't have a lab partner." She'd discovered not only her love for science, but her love for Matt Ross. "And so it began." But the memory of the beginning of their romance also reminded her of how it ended and she shifted her weight self-consciously off her bad hip. "That was a long time ago."

"Yes, it was."

Was that regret she saw in his eyes? But she rationalized he was only feeling the pull of nostalgia. Being back in your old high school after so long could bring back a slew of memories. Claire was used to them; she'd worked through them and managed to put them out of her mind most of the time. She had new memories at Lakeshore High, memories that included different kids from the ones she used to know and herself as teacher.

"How are things in the security office?" she asked, trying to keep both of them from following the path down memory lane. It was a route filled with too many land mines.

"Chaotic. I don't know who hired these guys, but they obviously haven't had the proper training or experience to be handling security for a school of this size. I worked up a list of some issues that needed to be addressed—starting with securing that door by the cafeteria—then sent them to handle it."

"We've never had much need for security."

"There's always a need for good security. Besides, given the massive drug ring operating out of Lakeshore, I'd have to disagree with you about that."

She cringed at that reminder. "How could this be happening right under our noses and no one knew it?"

"Criminal minds are used to operating around the norms so as not to raise suspicions. And the kids aren't going to talk because they don't want to lose their supplier. They have no idea how dangerous Trixie is."

"I wish I could do something."

"You did, Claire. You reached Luke. And he's the reason I'm here. It's because of you that we might have our first crack in this drug ring."

Although she appreciated him saying so, she knew it wasn't true. "All I wanted to do was to help Luke. Instead, I got him killed."

"His death isn't your fault. There are people who

are responsible for his death and for the dangerous substances flowing through this school, but I'll find out who they are and bring them to justice. Trust me. You keep doing your job and I'll do mine. And speaking of your job, what is this stuff you're cutting up?" He changed tracks so quickly that it took her a moment to catch up.

He pulled up a stool. "Tell me about it."

She held out the soft material. "It's called sodium metal. It's soft enough to cut with a knife." She filled a beaker full of water, then put on her safety glasses and handed a pair to Matt. "But when it comes in contact with water, it combusts." She dropped a small piece in the water and it bubbled and popped and smoked, giving about the same explosive reaction as a small firecracker. "I do this experiment every year. The kids seem to like it. I even have a video showing a university team that tossed a much larger quantity of sodium metal into a lake, then watched as it exploded, sending water spewing."

"Wow. That sounds amazing."

"It is fun. I hope it helps turn the students' attentions, even if briefly, from the tragedy of Luke's death."

He picked up a piece of the soft, malleable metal. "It's hard to believe this little piece of goop could cause such a reaction."

"Things aren't always what they seem. That's why I like chemistry. Something doesn't have to be big and bold to be strong. A chemical reaction isn't about strength and bulkiness. It's about what's on the inside. It's kind of like faith. You never know the true strength of someone until you mix it with something that causes a reaction."

He smiled at her, his hazel eyes shining. Being here with him seemed familiar and comfortable, and she felt her attraction to him flare into an unhealthy area—the memory of his whisper-soft touch and the sound of his heartbeat as she'd pressed her face into his chest. She pushed those kinds of thoughts away. She couldn't think of him that way anymore. Yes, he'd made her feel safe and protected, but the past was the past. He wasn't that same boy from high school any more than she was the same girl.

Instead, she turned her attention to the present. "I'll be glad to have the kids back in class tomorrow. Of course, I'll be operating out of a makeshift classroom, which isn't ideal, but I'm anxious to evaluate how they're coping with Luke's death."

"You really care about those kids, don't you?"

"It's why I became a teacher. These kids need someone to look after them, to nurture them. To see their potential and help develop it."

"That's nice, Claire."

Truly, teaching had been her lifeline when she was trying to rebuild her life after the accident. After the months and years of rehab and forcing herself to get up every day to acquire her degree. She'd had to fight for each and every accomplishment.

But Matt had not stuck around for that part. He'd left her broken emotionally and physically. He'd not been interested in a less-than-perfect girlfriend. Sure she'd forgiven him for not wanting her then and for not sticking around, but with him back she knew she had to guard her heart. She wouldn't let herself fall for him again. She'd worked too hard to rebuild her life only to have it shattered once more by his rejection.

She stood and rubbed her hip. It was stiff and painful after the past few days, and she knew her limp would be more pronounced than usual. Others might not notice, but Matt would. She felt the way his eyes looked at her, examining her, curious to discover how well she'd healed from her injuries. Perhaps he was looking to ease his guilt, but he needn't have worried. That was the past and this was the present and Claire knew there was no future for them together. She knew it… Now she just had to keep reminding herself of it until he was gone from her life again.

He must have sensed the change in her determination, or maybe it was the reminder of her injury, because he put down the metal and stood. "Well, I should get back. I'm working on background checks on all the faculty and staff, starting with Luke's teachers and those he had regular contact with."

"You really believe someone at the school killed Luke? I still find that hard to believe."

"I'm only going by what Luke told me. Someone inside this school is involved with this drug ring and I won't stop until I find out who."

She was touched by his determination to wipe out evil lurking in the hallways. They were both in the business of protecting kids, and she liked that. Again she felt that dizzying chemistry between them, bubbling and popping, readying for an explosion. She was glad he was leaving her classroom. She simply didn't trust herself with her own emotions when he was around.

She was so focused on Matt that she didn't even notice Principal Spencer standing in the doorway until he cleared his throat and both Matt and Claire turned to him. She felt her face redden at being caught in what, to her, seemed like an intimate moment. There was no denying the attraction between them and she was certain even Principal Spencer could sense it.

Thankfully, he didn't mention it as he entered. "I've spoken with the superintendent and we've decided to hold a school meeting tonight as a way for parents to come and express their feelings about what's happened as well as for us as school officials to reassure parents that their children are safe here."

"That sounds like a good idea," Claire said. She knew the community was overwhelmed with worry and grief for their children. This forum would give parents the opportunity to voice their concerns and receive reassurances before sending their kids back to school tomorrow.

"Six o'clock in the auditorium. I'd like for all teachers to be present." He glanced at Matt. "It would be good if you could come, too."

Matt nodded but turned his gaze back to Claire. "If Claire is going, I'll be there, too."

"Wonderful. Well, I'll leave you two to get back to…whatever it is you were doing." He quickly walked out.

"Well, I guess we know what we're doing tonight," Matt said. "What do you say we get an early supper before the meeting?"

She nodded. "That would be good."

"Well, then I guess I'd better let you finish what you're doing. And I have a stack of background checks to dig through."

She watched him leave, then turned back to her prep work. She was glad Matt was nearby, but she had to remember not to let him get too close. Her heart simply couldn't stand another of his rejections.

The school auditorium was packed that night. Claire caught the stares of her students' parents. All she saw were angry glances and worried expressions. Claire was glad Matt was here with her as they walked together to the front of the auditorium and took a seat.

Daryl Brown, another chemistry teacher, came and took the seat beside her. "These parents look ready to riot," he said, and Claire agreed.

"They're worried about their children. I suppose it's natural."

Daryl shook his head. "They're looking for someone to blame. In the absence of a suspect, they'll blame the most convenient person."

She realized where he was heading with his logic. "You mean me, don't you?"

He shrugged. "A female teacher meeting with a male student after school hours? You have to admit, it looks suspicious, Claire. If I were a parent, I would demand answers."

His blunt assertion surprised her, but she realized he was probably right. She glanced around again and suddenly felt the angry stares of hundreds of pairs of eyes boring into her back. She moved closer to Matt, and he stretched his arm across the back of her chair, not touching her but still giving her a sense of comfort and protection from the mass of people who might be looking to her for answers she didn't have.

Principal Spencer called the meeting to order and tried to maintain it as several of the parents jumped to their feet to express their outrage over the state of the school where they'd placed their kids' futures.

"How can we be assured our kids are safe when we send them to school?" one parent demanded.

"Who is watching out for our kids?" another asked.

Principal Spencer attempted to be heard over the outbursts. "We are working with the police to bring whoever committed this terrible crime to justice, but as you know the school was closed and the victim was on school property alone. I assure you we do everything we can to ensure the safety of our students while they are on campus. We've even gotten some help to over-haul our security measures." He scanned the crowd, then pointed at Matt. "Agent Ross, would you come up here please and recount some of the security changes you're implementing?"

Matt glanced at her and she could see he wasn't pleased about being put on the spot by Principal Spencer. But he stood and walked onto the stage. Principal Spencer handed him the microphone, then stepped away, giving him the floor.

"I heard he was murdered," someone shouted. "A murder in our school. And what have the police done to find the one responsible?"

"What was she doing here?" one mother demanded, pointing to Claire. "Why is a female teacher meeting alone with a male student on the weekend? Is that the kind of business going on at this school?"

Others joined in in attacking Claire verbally. She shrank under their gazes, then turned and saw Daryl's I-told-you-so look.

Matt tried to be heard above the outbursts, but even with a microphone it was difficult. Another parent called for her immediate dismissal and demanded Principal Spencer fire her on the spot. Claire got up and ran from the auditorium amid the deafening roar of parents screaming for her dismissal.

She pushed through the double doors into the quiet of the hallway. She took a deep breath and let it out. All she'd wanted was to help Luke; now it seemed she was on trial. She knew parents were frightened, but why had this become about her?

Lord, why is this happening to me?

She was content to let the meeting go forward without her; it was obvious she wasn't wanted there. She headed for the lab, where she could grade papers from last week while she waited for the meeting to end.

The light was on in the lab, which surprised her. She pushed open the door and saw the janitor's bucket in the middle of the room, but he was nowhere in sight. The supply cabinet door was ajar and she knew she'd locked it earlier.

She opened it and noticed several open containers. Someone had been in here. She knew from experience that the other science teachers always locked this cabinet. They all knew that some of the chemicals could be dangerous.

She closed the cabinet and secured the lock, but a sound behind her grabbed her attention. She turned and saw the mop was now on the floor. Had someone knocked it over? Or had it fallen on its own?

She looked around and saw no one but realized coming here alone had not been a smart move. She should have stayed close to Matt. She headed for the door, planning to go back to the safety of the crowd of people in the auditorium. Before she made it out the door, someone leaped from behind a lab station and grabbed her. He wore a black ski mask so she couldn't see his face, but he held a thick wire in his hand that she quickly realized was a power cord ripped from one of the microscopes on the lab station.

"Got you," he said, holding her secure so she couldn't run.

He pushed her up against the supply cabinet and wrapped the cord around her neck. She pulled at the cord as it tightened around her neck. He meant to kill her.

She kicked and pushed at him, but his grip didn't loosen. If only she hadn't gone off by herself. Everyone was in the auditorium and she knew no one would hear her over the shouting even if she could scream.

No one was coming to rescue her this time.

THREE

"This will teach you to meddle in my business," her attacker hissed at her, tightening his choke hold and ramming her head against the metal of the cabinet several times for good measure.

Blinding pain ripped through her and the room began to spin. She was going to lose consciousness and that would be the end of her...but she wasn't going down without a fight.

She pressed her hand against the cabinet and reached inside for the sodium metal. She felt the chunk she hadn't yet cut up. If she could reach the sink and fill it with water, she could toss the sodium into it and let the reaction stun her attacker long enough for her to escape. But the sink was across the room and she didn't think she would make it that far before losing consciousness even if she could wrangle free long enough.

But she could make it to the janitor's bucket and it was full of water.

Instead of the sodium, she grabbed the lighter from the cabinet, clicked it on and jabbed the hot edge against her attacker's neck. He grimaced with pain and knocked it from her hand, loosening his grip for a moment to do so. That was long enough for Claire. She shoved him, grabbed the sodium and tossed it, praying her target found its mark. He looked to see what she'd done and was rewarded with an explosion when the sodium contacted with the water. Her attacker screamed and covered his face where his mask was scorched by the explosion. Claire took advantage of his disorientation to push him and scramble away.

She ran out of the room and down the hall, dragging the long part of the cord behind her. She tried to scream for help, but her throat was raw and nothing escaped her lips but heavy sobs.

She spotted someone approaching and stopped suddenly, fear pulsing through her. Was it someone else coming after her?

The man called her name and rushed toward her, and Claire realized it was Matt coming to find her.

She fell into his arms the moment he was close enough. She couldn't speak but sobs racked her body. He pulled the cord from her neck and pushed back her hair that had fallen in her face. "What happened? Who did this?"

She took a deep breath and concentrated on forming words. "Couldn't see face. Mask." Her words were choppy and quick and it hurt like crazy to make the sounds come out, but at least she could speak. Another minute or two and she wouldn't have made it out of that lab alive.

Claire passed out in his arms.

"Call 9-1-1," Matt said, and several people who had emerged from the auditorium ready to leave reached for their phones.

He scooped her up and carried her to the couch in the teachers' lounge. The mark on her neck from the power cord was thick and dark and already turning a deep shade of purple. Matt grimaced at the sight of it and fear rustled through him. What if she hadn't been able to escape? What if the attacker had finished the job and killed her while he was trying to talk sense into a bunch of overindulgent parents justifying their overindulged kids? The idea tasted bitter in his mouth. He should never have allowed Spencer to lure him onto the stage. He'd let down his guard and Claire had nearly paid the ultimate price.

He pulled out his phone and dialed Preston's number. "It's Claire," he said when Preston answered. "She was attacked at the school."

Preston hesitated only a moment, then responded, "I'm on my way."

The police and ambulance were on their way and Claire would have to detail for the local police every moment from the time she'd left the auditorium. Was she up for that? She had to be.

She began to rouse, groaned in pain and tried to sit up. "What happened?" she whispered, her voice hoarse and raw.

He poured her a glass of water and handed it to her, then sat beside her on the couch. "You were attacked. Do you remember anything?"

She rubbed at the place on her neck. "I didn't see his face. He surprised me, but I did hear his voice. It sounded familiar but I can't place it."

The sound of the ambulance siren outside the window ended his questions. The EMTs rushed inside and began tending to Claire, and Matt gave them room to work. Preston entered the lounge and stared at Claire, his face paling at the sight of her.

"Are you okay?"

She nodded. "A little shaken up but okay."

He glanced at an EMT, who confirmed Claire's condition. "Her vitals are fine and there doesn't appear to be any long-term damage. I would like to transport her to the hospital for additional tests."

"I'm not going to the hospital," she insisted. "I'm fine."

Preston raked a hand over his face, then sat down beside her. "Tell me what happened."

She recounted going to the lab, having the cord wrapped around her neck and tossing the sodium metal into the janitor's bucket to cause the explosion and running as fast as she could toward the auditorium.

"I couldn't see his face because of the ski mask, but he said this would teach me not to meddle in his business."

Preston asked a few more questions, then stood. "I'll have my officers secure the lab. I'm going to go take a look at it. I'll check on you later," he told her before walking out.

Matt caressed her cheek, thankful to see her color was returning. "I'll be right back," he said, then stationed a security guard at the door and followed Preston to the lab.

Chairs and equipment had been knocked over. Water was spilled on the floor and the janitor's bucket was across the room under the window. But the most notable feature was the new blackened area on the wall by the supply cabinet. He remembered her explanation to him earlier in the day of the combustible nature of sodium metal.

Preston shook his head in disbelief, but Matt grinned, proud of the way Claire had fought against her attacker. "That ought to teach them not to mess with a chemistry teacher," he said proudly. Claire had always been a fighter and he was thankful to see that hadn't changed.

Preston flashed him a look that warned him this was no laughing matter.

By the time they returned to the lounge, Preston's agitation had grown. He turned to Claire. "I hope this attack shows you how dangerous it is for you to be here."

Anger flashed in her eyes and she unsteadily stood to face him. "I can't let these people win, Preston. Yes, they've threatened me and tried to hurt me, but they've also threatened my students. I won't back down until we uncover who is doing this."

Matt had never been more impressed with this woman's tenacity. He couldn't help but think she would have made a good ranger given her stubborn determination and persistence. She didn't give up.

And neither would he. He would find whoever had attacked Claire tonight and he would make them pay.

Claire shivered in her seat as Matt drove them back to the hotel.

"Are you cold?" he asked, reaching to adjust the heater.

She shook her head. It wasn't the chill in the air that bothered her as much as the realization that someone had meant to kill her tonight. Before, she could wave the threat away, insisting she wasn't a target, but now there was no doubt. Someone had followed her to the lab and tried to end her life.

Matt parked the car at the hotel, then shut off the engine. "Maybe you should have gone to the hospital."

"There's nothing they can do for me. I'm fine. I just want to feel safe again."

"I know this is difficult, but I promise you I'll do everything I can to keep you safe."

She was thankful for his supporting arm as they walked to their rooms. But suddenly she felt Matt tense as they approached the rooms. He stepped in front of her, but not before she saw her hotel room door ajar.

He reached under his jacket and pulled out his gun, ramping up Claire's tension.

"Wait here," he said, his voice husky and tense.

He pushed open the door, his gun drawn and his stance alert. She followed him inside and saw her clothes and belongings strewn across the room. Matt checked behind every door and into every cranny. He moved into the bathroom and she saw him pause, then glance her way.

"What is it?" she asked. Something was wrong. She saw it in his expression.

He put away his gun as she stepped toward the bathroom. She saw the color on the glass before she even entered. In lipstick, a message had been written across the mirror. *Don't get another student killed.*

Claire gasped, then turned away, right into Matt's arms. He felt her shiver again but this time knew it wasn't from the cold. He'd promised to keep her safe, yet in just the past few hours she'd been attacked and nearly choked to death and now had her room broken into and threatened.

One thing was for sure. They weren't safe here.

"Pack your things," he told her. "We're not staying here."

"Where are we going?"

"I'm taking you to my parents' house. My dad used to be a cop, remember? It's the only place I know you'll be safe."

Her eyes lit up briefly. "To your parents' house? Do you think they would mind?"

He had no doubt his family would be thrilled to see Claire again. His mother still hadn't forgiven him for not marrying her. "They'd love to have you." He wasn't so certain they would be thrilled with him, though, since they didn't even know he was in town.

"I would feel safer there," Claire said.

"Good, then it's settled."

He left the adjoining door open while they both packed up their belongings. He pulled out his cell phone and dialed his parents' number. He would have a lot of explaining to do, but he would shoulder it if it kept Claire safe.

Claire caught her breath as Matt turned the car into his parents' driveway. She suddenly felt seventeen again. How many hours had they spent hanging out at this house? How many times had she imagined his family were her family and dreamed about a future where it all came true?

The oldest of four kids, Matt came from a large,

close-knit family. Growing up as an only child, Claire had missed the warmth and familiarity of the Ross household. Her parents were both professionals who worked long hours, and Claire was often left on her own in the evenings. She'd fallen hard for Matt, but she'd fallen just as much in love with his family. So when he'd left her, she'd lost more than just the love of her life and hopes and dreams for a future. She'd lost family, too. Now she only saw them casually around town or at church and they spoke only in pleasantries, too much painful history separating them.

Until tonight, until Matt had brought her back into the fold.

But what would she do when he was gone again?

She tried not to focus on that. But her heart broke as she realized what she'd lost. And the pain was just as fresh and real as it had been ten years ago. Coming here tonight was reinforcing everything that stood between them.

"Claire? Are you okay?"

"I'm fine," she said, but even she heard the squeakiness of her voice. She got out of the car and let the night air pour over her. She couldn't lose control now, not here, not with Matt so close. She couldn't let him see how much he'd hurt her or how much she still grieved for all that was no longer hers. It had been years. She should be over it by now. She should have moved on with her life as Matt had, but she'd never been able to. Every man that she'd taken a chance on had been compared to Matt Ross and had failed to measure up. Despite the fact that he'd left her when she was no longer beautiful, when she was battered and broken and crippled, she'd never gotten over him.

He got out and walked around the car toward her. "Claire?"

She shuddered at the sound of her name. How could she still be pining for a man who'd left her when she needed him most? Who hadn't loved her enough to love her as a cripple? Preston was right when he'd said Matt Ross didn't deserve her. And she didn't deserve the heartache that would come when he left again.

She pushed away that emotion. She wouldn't give him the satisfaction of seeing how he still affected her. "I'm fine." But she couldn't keep the jitteriness out of her voice when she spoke.

"You've been through a lot today. It's normal to be overwhelmed. I would be surprised if you weren't. The Claire Kendall I knew was too tenderhearted not to let today's events affect her."

She glared at him, suddenly angry that he presumed to know anything about her. She might still be harboring unhealthy feelings for him, but that didn't mean she was the same girl he'd walked out on all those years ago. "You think you know me, Matt? The Claire Kendall you knew died ten years ago in that car on prom night. You have no idea who I am now because you never bothered to stick around to find out. So don't pretend to know me, because you don't."

His face was stoic as he nodded, then picked up her suitcase. "You're right. I'm sorry. I'll take you inside."

He popped open his trunk and pulled out a small garment bag. He hesitated before closing the trunk, but Claire noticed.

"How long has it been since you've been home?" He shrugged. "Quite a while."

She remembered the Ross family as extremely close and loving. "When was the last time you saw your parents?"

"They visited me in the hospital last year after my ranger unit was ambushed. That was the last time."

Ambushed? Hospitalized?

Claire shuddered at those words and all they implied. She'd been afraid to ask why he'd left the rangers, afraid it was something like this.

"I didn't know about the ambush. I'm sorry. Were you badly injured?"

"I cracked several vertebrae during a firefight. The fractures healed, but I still have some residual nerve damage, which made continuing on as a ranger difficult. I had a former commander who knew someone in the DEA's office, so he helped me get my foot in the door there."

But hearing that he hadn't seen his family in over a year broke her heart. She knew she'd lost contact with the Ross family, but this was their own son. She hadn't realized how infrequently he'd returned home in the years since the accident. She'd always assumed he came and left town without her being aware, but now she realized how naive that was. Lakeshore wasn't that large a town. She should have heard something about Matt's visits, but she hadn't because he hadn't made any. Was it because of her? Was it one more consequence of that terrible night so long ago?

Matt hugged his dad as his parents met them at the front door. He kissed his mom, then carried their bags inside. Papa Ross gave Claire a bear hug that reminded her of better days when they referred to her as their almost daughter. But even that memory was painful. She thanked them both for allowing her to stay.

"You're always welcome here, Claire," Papa Ross assured her. "We have a state-of-the-art alarm system, and someone is always home. You'll be safe."

Mama Ross put her arm around Claire. "I made up the guest room for you. It's Danny's old room right across from Alisa. She's staying with a friend tonight."

Alisa, Matt's youngest sister, was the one getting married in two weeks. She was living out the dream Claire and Matt had once shared for themselves.

"No one will disturb you," Mama Ross said. "You sleep as late as you like and I'll save some breakfast for you."

"Thank you for the offer, but I have class tomorrow."

Matt looked at her, concerned. "Claire, you're going to school tomorrow?"

"I have to."

"You were nearly killed tonight. Are you sure you want to go back there?"

"Luke's death has been all over the news. The kids know, so I need to be there to comfort them as best I can even if they just need to talk." Being there for her students was important to her. They would be confused and distraught about Luke's death. And Principal Spencer was still planning to reopen the school tomorrow, which meant students would be there. She had to be there, too.

"You're not safe there. I think that was proven tonight."

"I'll be fine. Nothing is going to happen to me while

school is in session. The campus will be swarming with kids. Whoever is behind this wouldn't dare risk trying to harm me in front of them."

He finally gave up his objections, and she walked upstairs to the bedroom Mama Ross had fixed for her. Matt didn't understand her need to be there for her students, but it was important to her. She'd failed Luke, but she was determined not to fail her students again. But despite her bravado in front of Matt, once the door was closed, she couldn't stop the tears she cried into her pillow.

Sleep didn't come easily for Matt that night. His mind was actively trying to connect the pieces of what had happened. Did the shooting at Claire's house have anything to do with her dead student? And the attack in the lab? It seemed too coincidental not to be related. What had Claire gotten herself involved in?

But it was her words to him in the yard that had left him feeling sucker punched. Nothing she'd said had been untrue. He didn't really know her anymore. Ten years could change a person in ways no one could have imagined. He was living proof of that. But he couldn't believe that Claire could have changed so much that the girl he'd known and loved wasn't still there inside of her.

Claire was right. He was being presumptuous. She'd been through years of rehabilitation and therapy. He'd read up on her injury and knew the kind of treatments she would have had to endure over the past years to get to where she was now. He'd only been living with nerve damage for over a year and some days it was nearly unbearable. He couldn't imagine the kind of pain she'd been dealing with for over ten years. In fact, very little evidence of the accident remained. Strangers would never know she'd been through anything. But she had and she'd gone through it alone. If only he'd been there. If only he hadn't run away like a frightened little boy. If only she had let him prove that his love hadn't ended that night all those years ago.

He should have pushed harder when she'd refused to see him. He should have hung on until her anger subsided. He knew now he'd given in too easily. He'd allowed his guilt and her rejection to drive him away from the only woman he'd ever loved.

Giving up on the notion of sleep, Matt crawled out of bed. He went into the living room and saw his parents at the dining room table huddled together as if they were engrossed in a deep discussion. He didn't have to wonder long if he was the topic of their late-night confab. When they saw him, they both straightened and got quiet.

"Still up, I see," Matt said, walking to the kitchen and pouring himself a mug full of the warm milk on the stove. He noticed his folks each had a mug of it in front of them. He joined them at the table, certain they had questions they needed to ask. He just hadn't decided yet if he was up to answering them.

His mother touched his shoulder, concern pouring over her face. "How are you?"

"I'm okay," he said, trying to reassure her, and for the most part it was true. He had his good days and his bad days, but his job at the DEA had helped to keep his mind occupied and away from the events of that terrible night on an Afghan mountain.

His father was more direct. "What are you doing with Claire, Matt?"

Matt was taken aback by his abruptness about Claire. He'd expected them to question him about the ambush, his new job, why he hadn't been home in years, not to focus on Claire. "I told you when I phoned she was in danger. I guess you've seen the news about the boy who was murdered at the high school?"

They both nodded that they'd seen the coverage.

"It was one of Claire's students, a boy named Luke Thompson." He went through again how Luke had contacted him and brought him to Lakeshore for a meeting. "Luke never told me who he was working for, so I have no idea who is after Claire, but someone wants to find out what she knows or make sure she can't repeat it."

"You're playing with fire by bringing her here."

"I couldn't just walk away from her. Not again. Luke might still be alive were it not for my involvement in his life, and by extension Claire wouldn't be in danger."

His father gazed at him knowingly. "Is that what this is about? You're feeling guilty?"

"I have a lot to make up for. I won't let anything happen to her. I won't." Although his family knew about the ambush, he'd never talked to them about it and they hadn't pushed him, but they had to know he was thinking about those in his ranger squad who were killed. "I've lost too many people I care about already. I won't lose another."

The events of the past two days had worn her down. Claire stared in the mirror the next morning trying to cover the dark circles of worry and lack of sleep with makeup.

She finished dressing—having chosen a shirt with a collar to hide the ugly mark on her neck—but hesitated about going downstairs. She could already hear movement as the Rosses gathered for breakfast. She hadn't thought this through enough. She hadn't thought about having to face this family—this family she once loved so much. It stabbed at her heart to know she was here but she was no longer a part of them and never would be.

For years, she'd kept a slip of paper containing a Bible verse pinned to the inside of her makeup bag for occasions such as this morning when she was feeling down on herself—a reminder that it didn't matter what others thought of her, only what God thought of her and that God loved her. She had to remind herself of that constantly. It had been easier in the beginning when she was fighting and determined to reclaim her independence, but now years later the lingering effects of the wreck still bothered her, reminding her that she was damaged goods. She could always pep herself up enough to get through the day, but today one of the few people who would notice the catch in her step was here and she had to face him.

She took a deep breath, closed her eyes and repeated the words. "God loves me just the way I am." She shut her makeup bag, grabbed her books and purse and marched downstairs before the doubt had time to creep back.

"Claire!" Alisa squealed and ran to her, nearly tipping her over as she wrapped her arms around Claire for a hug. "It's so good to see you."

"You, too, Alisa. Congratulations on your upcoming marriage."

"Thank you. His name is David and he is wonderful." She linked her arm through Claire's and marched her toward the dining room. "I would ask how you are, but my brother has been filling us in on all that's happened. It's terrible about your student. You must have been terrified."

"Yes, I was. If Matt hadn't arrived when he did…" She glanced at the man who'd saved her life twice already and suddenly her heart fluttered. He didn't look the least bit sleep-deprived. In fact, he looked clean-shaven, vibrant and ready to take on the day. And gorgeous. His eyes twinkled as he sipped his coffee and smiled at her. Claire had to admit he looked amazing.

He leaned down to ask her a question and Claire caught the scent of his aftershave that left her a little light-headed.

"How did you sleep?"

She decided not to mention her restlessness. Surely they could see it on her face. "Fine." She poured herself a cup of coffee, hoping it was nice and strong.

Mama Ross set a plate of pancakes in front of her and Claire started to protest.

"Don't you dare," Mama told her. "You look like you haven't had a good breakfast in ages. You'll need the energy to get through the day."

She glanced around at them all eating, suddenly remembering Mama Ross loved to cook for her family and they loved to eat. She smiled thinking that had she married Matt ten years ago, she probably would have been big as a house by now.

She said a quick blessing, then cut into the blueberry pancakes and was awed by the flavor and the taste of Mama Ross's cooking. She would definitely have been plump by now as Matt's wife... Plump but happy.

Matt smiled at the image of Claire mingling with his family but his enjoyment faded quickly. This was how it should have been, but he'd ruined it.

"Excuse me," he said, getting up and carrying his plate into the kitchen. He leaned into the counter and tried to catch himself. Seeing Claire like this was a constant reminder of all he'd lost and his biggest mistake ever. He didn't like to think about that. He didn't like mistakes. They made you weak and Matt had spent his life making certain he wasn't weak again.

His mother entered the kitchen and gave him a curious look. "Are you okay?"

He nodded and began rinsing off his plate.

Still, she stared. "Is it your back? Is it paining you this morning?"

His spine injury from the ambush caused his back to constantly hurt him. That along with shooting nerve pain had been his main factor in leaving the rangers. He simply couldn't count on his fitness any longer. "I'm fine. I was just catching my breath."

His mother glanced into the dining room, then gave him a knowing smile. "It's hard seeing her here, but I have missed her smile."

Matt stared out at Claire and the big grin that brightened her face as she listened to Alisa tell her all about her fiancé. He'd missed it, too.

But he didn't have time to focus on the past. He had a killer to find in the here and now and he wouldn't rest until he knew Claire was safe. He wouldn't let her down again.

Claire glanced at the clock. "We should go," she told Matt. "I want to be there when the kids start to arrive."

Once in his car and on the way, the awkward silence between them was deafening. He thought about what Claire had told him last night and realized she was right. He knew nearly nothing about her from the past ten years.

"So you never married?" he asked her.

She blushed and shook her head. "You?"

"I had the job. I always had the job." No point in admitting that no one had ever compared to her. "It didn't seem right to commit to a relationship when I traveled so much with the rangers."

"Preston and I went on a cruise two summers ago. The water was beautiful. That's the only traveling I've ever done."

He grimaced. Was it possible he'd misinterpreted their relationship? Preston certainly seemed to believe there was more to it than friendship. But who was he to question her about her love life? He had no right… but he had to know for sure.

"Are you and Preston together?"

"He's a good friend."

So she was the delusional one. Preston obviously wanted more than friendship. "I don't recognize him from around town. He didn't grow up in Lakeshore, did he?"

"No, he's from Nashville. He came here five years ago when a job opened up on the police force. We met when he pulled me over for speeding."

"He wrote you a ticket?"

"He did, but when I went to pay the ticket, he offered to tear it up if I would have coffee with him, so I did. We've been friends ever since."

She was oblivious to the effect she had on men. Her bubbly personality drew people to her. That was probably why she made a good teacher. That and her kindness and compassion and desire to help in any way she could.

She was so utterly beautiful in her innocence.

He pulled into the school lot and saw it was already much busier than yesterday. He parked in the teachers' lot and saw her hesitate as she reached for the door handle. "Are you sure you're up for this?"

She took a deep breath, then smiled. "I have to be."

"You said it yourself. No one is going to try to harm you while school is in session." He wasn't sure he believed it, but he could see she needed to.

She nodded and got out. He could tell she was still skeptical, but she forged ahead because she knew it was what the kids needed. He admired her for her courage and also for her dedication. She wasn't paying lip service to these kids. She truly cared about them.

He wished he was as confident of that as he hoped he sounded. He wouldn't have thought someone would attack her last night, either, but they had. He had plans to stay close to her today, as close as possible without stepping on her toes.

He'd worked out a plan to have the security staff monitor the halls more frequently and with a greater presence. It was important that the students and faculty felt safe in order to get things back to normal, but an increased show of security would also apply pressure to anyone trying to push drugs. Add that to his DEA presence and Matt knew whoever Luke's supplier was would be getting edgy. And that meant he was more likely to make a mistake that would lead Matt right to Luke's killer.

Preston was waiting for him outside the security office. Matt noticed crime scene tape over the door of the lab only a few rooms down.

"Did your team find anything that might lead us to who attacked Claire?"

"Our team is still processing the evidence collected last night, but you were right about Luke. The coroner ruled time of death between noon and 2:00 p.m., meaning there's no way he sent that text. We've confirmed with the cell carrier the time it was sent and the time it was received. There's no discrepancy."

Matt felt that like a punch to the gut. "Claire was a target."

"It sure looks that way. Whoever killed Luke either wanted her to find him or planned to kill her, too."

"Maybe not. Their intent could have been as simple as finding out if Luke confided any information about their operation to her."

"Well, after last night, I'd say they've decided killing her might be the best option."

"Does the report say how he died?"

"Yep." Preston handed him the file. "The coroner determined the murder weapon was a six-inch blade, probably a kitchen knife. The victim's throat was slashed from behind, but it wasn't a clean cut. Luke definitely bled out for a while before he died."

Which meant the killer stood around and watched

Luke die before setting the trap for Claire. And this was the twisted mind now targeting Claire.

"We didn't recover the knife, so my guess is the killer took it with him. I'm going to keep Claire's classroom sealed, along with the lab, but I've told Principal Spencer the rest of the hall can be opened up for students."

"Claire set up class in the auditorium. I'm doing background checks on all the staff and faculty at Lakeshore High. Luke hinted to me his supplier was someone on the inside. But I'll also need access to your local records of drug arrests." Trixie was a newer drug but was still a major player in the drug market and growing fast among the younger crowd. Schools were being flooded with it, which indicated a centralized manufacturing and distribution. If he could link a faculty member with past drug use, he might find his way in.

Preston looked skeptical. "The coroner found no evidence of illegal drugs in the initial toxicology report, so right now the only evidence we have that Luke's death was because of drugs is your word and Claire's word."

Matt thought Preston was about to balk at helping him investigate this path, but he sighed wearily and continued.

"Unfortunately, we've got no other leads. I'll start running down names for drug arrests and send you the relevant ones."

Matt nodded. "I've also looked through the interviews your officers conducted and flagged a few for follow-up interviews. I'll concentrate on that today."

Preston started to leave, then turned back to him. "How is she this morning?"

Matt saw the look of concern on his face and knew he cared for her. "She's Claire—stubborn to the core and determined to be here for her students."

Preston nodded solemnly, probably thinking of last night. "Yes, she is stubborn. One day, it's going to get her killed," he stated bluntly as he walked away.

Claire pushed back the doubts and the accusation and tried to focus on the kids, already arriving and still in shock over Luke's death. She spent several hours talking with them, sometimes one-on-one and sometimes in groups. Most of them only wanted to be with the other kids. Words were few and the mood on campus was somber.

Claire was glad the police hadn't released the news about Luke's drug use or about the circumstances of his death. She suspected most of the kids already knew about his business—many were probably the ones he sold to—but today was all about the Luke they all knew. The well-liked, popular student who had died tragically way too young.

Claire was emotionally and physically drained by two o'clock. Many of the kids had left the campus and the crowd in the parking lot was thinning. She decided to take the time to move supplies again, this time to her new, makeshift classroom in the auditorium.

But as she walked through the outside courtyard tucked between the parking lot and the cafeteria, she heard her name being called.

"Miss Kendall?"

Claire turned to find one of her students, Jessica

Alvarez, behind her. The girl's eyes were red from crying and she held a tissue in her hand.

"Jessica, you're still here?"

"I was hoping I could talk to you."

"Sure." Claire led her toward a bench and they sat down. "How are you holding up?"

"I can't believe he's really dead," the girl said. She glanced around, her eyes cutting each way. "I know Luke trusted you, Miss Kendall. He said you were someone he could turn to."

Her heart warmed at hearing that Luke had believed in her. If only she'd been able to save him. "I wish I could have done more to help him."

Jessica twisted her hands nervously. Something more than grief seemed to be affecting her. The way she kept fidgeting and looking around the area as she spoke. Jessica seemed afraid. Claire supposed that was normal, too, since a violent crime had occurred on campus.

She reached for the girl's hand. "You're safe here, Jessica. No one is going to harm you."

Jessica cast her eyes around again and started to speak, but then her face froze and she went pale. "I have to go," she said quickly. Claire saw her glance back as she walked away, but it wasn't Claire she was looking at. It was someone behind her. Claire turned to see. A few students were still gathered in groups and she spotted Principal Spencer and several teachers milling about speaking with them.

Claire wanted to rush after Jessica and find out what was going on with her and how she could help. Jessica and Luke hadn't been that close that Claire knew of. She'd never seen them together at school.

But these kids often formed alliances and friendships that she knew nothing about. Luke had told Jessica that Claire was someone he could turn to for help, and Claire was glad that Jessica had reached out to her. She just wished Jessica had stuck around to let her help.

Her cell phone rang and Claire glanced at the screen and saw that Matt was calling.

"Where are you, Claire? I came by the auditorium to check on you and you're not there."

"I'm outside in the courtyard." She could hear the panic in his voice and knew she'd worried him. She hadn't missed the multiple times he'd passed by her door today or the increased security she'd seen around the school. She, for one, felt safer with him there. "I got distracted by a student."

"I see you."

She glanced around and spotted him across the courtyard. He grinned and waved to her. She couldn't help but smile. Sometimes it seemed as if he was still the Matt she'd known and they'd never been apart.

She stepped off the curb and walked across the parking lot toward him. Suddenly, she heard Matt yell simultaneously through the phone and across the yard. The screech of tires and the roar of an engine grabbed her attention. She turned to find a truck barreling toward her. Her feet were frozen and all she saw was the grille aiming right at her. She was going to die.

Suddenly, someone grabbed her arm and yanked her out of the way. Her knee dug into the concrete as she fell and her shoulder smashed into the ground, causing pain to erupt through her.

The tires of the truck screeched to a halt, but the truck tapped the concrete blocker before it turned and sped away.

She glanced up at the man who had saved her life. She was in Matt's arms again and relief flooded her. She never wanted to be anywhere else.

FOUR

Claire felt small but safe in his arms, but eventually Matt had to let her go. The police and the ambulance arrived, and Matt left Claire to them while he gave his statement, then helped question the remaining students.

Few of them had seen the truck that had tried to run down Claire, but he had—a black pickup truck with tinted windows and a red sticker of some kind in the window. The afternoon sun had blocked his view of the driver's face, but he'd made out a man wearing a baseball cap pulled down low with dark sunglasses hiding his face. Matt knew their best chance was going to be to find that truck, which would hopefully lead them to the driver.

Claire wasn't the only one traumatized by the incident. He looked around and noticed several female students sobbing and being comforted. The students and faculty were already under pressure after Luke's death, and now this added near miss would shake anyone. Fortunately, most of the students had already left campus for the day.

He approached the ambulance and saw Claire with

a sling on her arm. The paramedic was tending to scrapes on her knee and her slacks were torn on the leg.

"How are you?" he asked her.

She flashed him a half smile, but he saw pain in her lovely eyes and fatigue lining her face. "I'll be fine. My shoulder was jarred, but they don't think anything is broken."

The EMT raised his head at her comment. "We would like to transport her to the hospital for scans just in case."

She shook her head. "I'm fine."

But Matt insisted she listen to the professionals. "It won't hurt to have the scans, just to be sure."

She started to argue but was cut off by the sound of a blaring siren approaching. Preston's car skidded to a stop and he leaped out, leaving the door standing open. He rushed to the ambulance, his face pale and stricken.

"Claire! Are you injured? What happened?"

"I'm fine," she said, laying a hand on his arm, which Matt didn't miss—and didn't like one iota.

Preston touched her face, staring too deeply for Matt's liking into her eyes. "I'm sorry I wasn't here sooner. I was on the other side of town dealing with a robbery call. I didn't hear this had happened until I was through at that scene. Why didn't you call me?"

She looked flustered as she glanced his way, so Matt stepped in. He could sense she didn't want to tell Preston that she'd been too wrapped up in his arms to find her phone. "One of the students called 9-1-1. Claire was pretty shaken up."

That was the understatement of the century. She'd been terrified. She'd been targeted. Was it because of Luke? The timing seemed too coincidental not to be. Had Luke told her all his secrets during those counseling sessions she'd claimed to have had with him? Had he given her the name of his supplier or hinted at it? If Matt was asking these questions, then he was certain Luke's supplier was, as well. Had they really meant to run her down today? Or had it been a ploy like the drive-by to warn her to keep her mouth shut?

His muscles tensed. Even if they were trying to scare her into silence, they would still want to find out what she knew, and that meant trouble for Claire. If they abducted her and interrogated her about what Luke had told her, no way would they let her go after that. They'd killed Luke because he wanted out of the business, so they obviously had no qualms about killing. They might decide to kill Claire just to make sure she couldn't talk, regardless of what she knew.

He had to get to the bottom of this. He had to find out who Luke's supplier was and who was behind the drug ring operating at Lakeshore. Claire's life depended on him uncovering the guilty party.

"The paramedics want her to go to the hospital," Matt told Preston. "But she's refusing."

"Don't be ridiculous, Claire. Go to the hospital. I'll be right behind you," Preston told her.

"Me, too," Matt said. "I think we'd both feel better if you went."

She finally allowed the EMT to load her into the ambulance, but Matt had one last question before they closed the doors.

"Do you know anyone at the school who drives a black pickup truck?"

She thought for a moment, then shook her head. "I don't think so. I didn't get a good look at the truck, but it didn't look familiar."

When the ambulance pulled away, Preston turned on Matt. "You were supposed to protect her." It was more an accusation than a question, and Matt felt his face flush. He'd reached Claire before the truck that had tried to run her over. He would call that protecting her.

"I gave my statement to one of the officers." Maybe others could claim not to remember. The rush of action often obscured memories for those who weren't used to it, but Matt had been a ranger, was still a ranger at heart, and he'd been in worse action before. He'd been trained during his time as an army ranger to observe and react in high-intensity situations. He'd also been trained to keep his wits about him, and he'd always been good at compartmentalizing things. He'd been good at seeing past the action and looking to the truth of the matter. But today, emotion had nearly overwhelmed him at the fear of losing this lady again. She may never want to have anything to do with him again as far as romance was concerned after the way he'd left her, but he couldn't imagine a world where Claire Kendall didn't exist. And he didn't want to be part of a world where she wasn't around anymore.

Most of all, he'd promised her she would be safe at school and she wasn't. He'd failed to protect her again.

"If you can't protect her, then you need to step aside," Preston said before getting into his unmarked police car and taking off.

Matt climbed into his own car and followed behind

him to the hospital. His pulse was racing and he knew he had to calm down. His hands gripped the steering wheel so tight his fingers began to whiten from lack of blood. He would be no good to Claire if he couldn't pull himself together and focus on the investigation.

His phone buzzed in the holder and he saw Garrett's name on the caller ID. Garrett Lewis was a fellow former army ranger and a friend. He quickly accepted the call, needing something else to occupy his thoughts right now.

"Hey, Garrett, what's up?"

"I'm leaving the country in a few weeks and so I was trying to tie up loose ends before I go…one of which is getting a wedding gift. Do you know what you're getting them?"

"Not yet." Josh Adams, another of his former ranger squad buddies, was marrying Elise Richardson, an FBI agent who'd uncovered a human trafficking ring that had kidnapped Josh's niece. Their wedding was still a few months away and he'd been focused on getting through his sister's wedding before thinking about Josh's. Now he was only thinking about keeping Claire safe.

"Whatever I get I'll be sure to add your name to," Matt said. "You can pay me later."

"Great. Thanks, Matt."

"So what's this about you leaving the country? Where are you going?"

Garrett hesitated and Matt knew that wasn't a good sign.

"Where, Garrett?"

"Pakistan."

"What? Why?"

"I've got a job."

"What job? For who?"

"Colton has all the specs."

Terrific. Colton was as reckless as Garrett. Only, he was old enough to know better. "I don't like you leaving the country. It's not a good time."

"It never is." Garrett's tone indicated that he thought Matt was being overprotective again.

He couldn't help it. Garrett, five years his junior, was like a kid brother to him. He didn't like the risks Garrett and Colton took, and he liked even less the situations they often found themselves in. After leaving the rangers, they'd started doing freelance, privately funded search and rescue missions together.

Garrett ended up placating him long enough to get him off the phone, but Matt knew his worries went in one ear and out the other. One day, that boy was simply going to disappear and no one would ever know what happened to him. "Be careful," Matt told him. "And don't forget to check in."

"I won't forget," Garrett said, but then agitation seemed to fall from his tone. "Are you okay? You sound rattled, which is really weird for you."

"I'm fine," Matt assured him, but his hands were still shaking from the adrenaline rush. "I'll be fine."

He said goodbye and hung up with Garrett before his prodding continued. Matt was thankful for the support of his ranger brothers, but he wasn't comfortable letting them see him rattled. After the wreck, he'd become an expert at compartmentalizing and had gained a reputation among his squad as coolheaded. They'd even nicknamed him The Machine because of his lack of emotional response.

He wished now for some of that compartmentalization. He couldn't seem to do it when it came to Claire. His emotions were right on the edge, ready and available to let loose at any moment.

Matt pulled into the hospital parking lot and cut the engine. Unlike many of his ranger brothers, Matt had never married. No one could ever compare to his Claire, and he'd never desired to replace her. He'd often insisted he had family, and he did. He had a large family that loved him and would be devastated if something had happened to him while with the rangers. But his siblings were grown up now and marrying off to start families of their own, and his parents wouldn't always be around. One day soon, he might be truly alone. But he had no one in his life romantically and he never had for long.

He'd already met the love of his life and lost her.

Claire grimaced in pain as the technician manipulated her arm and shoulder to the right spot for the CT scan. Tears welled in her eyes but not because of the pain her injury caused. It was because of how she'd humiliated herself in front of Matt. She'd clung to him for too long before he'd had to pry her away so he could go investigate the scene.

Embarrassment rushed to her face as she remembered the look of revulsion in his expression as he walked away from her. She had to remember not to be so needy. She didn't want him to think she was still dependent and crippled.

She closed her eyes and tried to concentrate on her breathing, but her thoughts kept wandering to those moments in Matt's arms and how protected she'd felt with them wrapped around her. She felt safe with him. She tried to tell herself it was because of his experience as an army ranger. But Preston wanted to protect her, too. Why didn't she feel that same way about him? He'd tried to offer her comfort, yet it hadn't given her the same sense of security and assurance that she felt with Matt.

She shoved those memories away. They didn't matter anymore. Matt was only with her, only safeguarding her, because of her involvement with Luke. At the thought of Luke, tears threatened again. The CT technician smiled at her. "All done. I'll take you back to the ER."

As the tech wheeled her in a wheelchair—he'd insisted despite Claire's insistence that she could walk—they rounded the corner and she noticed Matt and Preston standing guard on opposite sides of the hall. They both looked agitated and angry.

Matt saw her and his face fell. "Claire, I'm sorry. I shouldn't have left you even for a moment. I should have stayed with you."

"You can't be with me all the time. I have classes to teach."

"Not anymore. From this point on you're on medical leave until we find out who's behind this."

She stared up at him, anger biting through her that he assumed he could command her to do something and she would do it. She stood to face him.

"I have students who need me. I won't let them down by cowering and hiding."

"Claire, these kids are conspiring against you. They must know Luke was selling drugs and they know you're in danger. Still, they've kept quiet. Why haven't they come forward to help you?"

"Because they're kids, Matt. They're scared and probably worried about getting into trouble. Don't you remember what it was like when you were a kid? When you messed up? How frightened you were of getting into trouble?"

He knew she was referring to the night of the wreck.

"Well, they'll have to talk to me," he said. "I'm starting student interviews tomorrow."

"Let me be there when you talk with them. They'll open up to me."

"No," Preston stated. "If whoever is behind Luke's death learns that you're asking questions, you could be in even more danger."

She turned to Preston. She knew he was only trying to look out for her, but his words rubbed her wrong. "Luke is dead. My house has been shot up and I've been choked, threatened and nearly run down. How could I possibly be in more danger?"

"Claire—"

"I'm doing this, Preston."

Preston raked a hand over his face but nodded his agreement. She looked at Matt and saw the same expression of resignation on his face.

They might not like it, but they wouldn't try to stop her again.

Claire had always had a stubborn streak. Matt was glad to see that hadn't changed. Despite Preston's agitation, she was determined to go back to school and be there for her students. He admired her determination and her loyalty, but Preston was right. She was walking into danger by stepping back into that school.

As they drove back to his parents' house, Matt tried to reassure her.

He remembered all too well the fear and worry after the wreck. Even through his worry about Claire and her injuries, he'd been terrified of the consequences he might face. They'd both been drinking and he'd been driving, a stupid, youthful mistake. He remembered worrying about going to jail, being questioned by the police and sitting with his dad in the lawyer's office. He'd even been afraid of the reaction of his family…the look of disappointment on his parents' faces when they'd arrived at the hospital. But that had been useless worry. Yes, there had been disappointment, but their faces had been full of fear and relief and anguish as they'd wrapped him in their arms and praised God for his safety.

Facing Claire's parents had been different. Their cold, angry stares had bored into him, blaming him for their daughter's predicament. And they were right to blame him. But that hadn't taken away the sting.

Claire was probably right that her students would be feeling something similar, afraid to come forward and face the consequences of what they'd been involved in. A boy was dead and that was a heavy burden for a teenager to bear.

They would be too afraid to talk to him openly. But they trusted Claire. They knew her. And most important, Luke had trusted her. If they had any chance of uncovering Luke's supplier, Claire needed to question those kids.

"During my quiet time, I've been reading the story

of Joseph in the Bible," she said, "and I see a lot of similarities between Joseph and kids today. Joseph was a favored son. He was given everything and favored by his father over his brothers. And after the dream he had about his brothers serving him, he was cocky and arrogant and overindulged. These kids are given everything they desire and many of them have no humility. They're not bad kids, they're just pampered, and I'm afraid, like Joseph, it can only bring them suffering eventually."

"Unless they have someone like you looking out for them."

Excitement shone in her beautiful eyes. "Matt, this could work. You have to trust me."

With almost anything else, he would have no problem trusting her, but she wasn't trained for this and she'd already become a target. If this afternoon proved anything, it was that Claire wasn't even safe at the school.

She obviously saw he was struggling with this, and instead of demanding she was going to do it no matter what, her face softened and she placed her hand softly on his arm in an effort, obviously, to scramble his thoughts. It worked.

"The past two days have been insane, and I would be crazy to try to convince you I'm not scared. The truth is I'm terrified. Someone killed Luke and now they're trying to kill me, too. I'm no fool. Of course I'm scared. But I'm not alone in this and that gives me confidence."

"I can't protect you if you won't let me—"

"I wasn't talking about you, Matt. I was talking

about God. He's always with me and my future, whatever it is, rests in His hands."

He fixed a hard stare on her, taken aback by her words. A Glock might make him feel better, but God?

"You used to believe in God," she said. "When we were kids, you had an incredible faith in God. What happened?"

Car wreck? Ambush? Dead friends? Lost the love of my life? Take your pick. "I grew up, Claire. I realized God didn't care about a dumb soldier from Tennessee."

"That's not true. He does care, Matt."

He shook his head, not wanting the course of this discussion to continue. He wasn't up for having a discussion on faith while they were dealing with a menace trying to kill them. His only care right now was keeping Claire safe, and that didn't include letting her go unprotected to school.

But what choice did he have but to trust her? She was right. By now, everyone had seen him on the news at the crime scene. It was a small town and everyone who knew his parents knew he was now working for the DEA. The students wouldn't talk with him, but they might open up for Claire.

He gave a resigned sigh as he realized he was going to let this happen. He needed it to happen. "I want you to promise me that you'll let me take the lead. You're only there to reassure the kids."

She nodded. "I understand."

"We'll go over some things tonight if you feel up to it." He turned to look at her, remembering her arm was in a sling and they'd just left the ER. She might need a night to recuperate before stepping into this hornet's nest.

"Tonight is fine," she said, causing Matt to smile.

Stubborn to the core, just as he remembered.

Matt had flagged several interviews the local police had conducted that he wanted to follow up on. They included Luke's closest friends and girlfriend. These were the people who would know about his extracurricular activity. Did they also have in-depth information about his supplier?

He set up in the security office. Claire looked tired but determined. She'd wanted to wear a high collar to hide the mark on her neck, but he'd encouraged her not to. It was better for the kids to see it as well as the sling on her arm. They needed to be reminded that something bad had happened in their school so they could understand the seriousness of the situation. Claire was a well-liked teacher, and Matt hoped seeing her in pain would help drop their guard.

Ryan Summerhold was first on the list. According to his own statement to the police, he and Luke had been best friends since kindergarten. Who better to know what Luke was up to than his best friend? But Matt knew he had to be wary. If Luke was involved with the drug ring, it was possible Ryan was, as well.

Ryan was a tall, slim, good-looking kid who paled when he saw Claire. He seemed anxious, but between having his best friend murdered and being questioned by the police and DEA, it would've been odd if he wasn't.

Matt offered him the chair opposite Claire. He wanted Ryan to see her and understand the enormity of what had happened. He sat on the desk, elevated above the boy. He wasn't trying to scare him, but a little intimidation often resulted in a quicker, honest response.

"Are you okay, Miss Kendall?" Ryan asked as he sat down.

Matt had prepared her for such a question and waited for Claire's response. He needed her to be honest and forthright. This was her first opportunity to do so, and Matt wondered if she would remember what they'd discussed. These interviews were important, and if Claire was going to be a part of them—which he wanted her to be—he needed her to follow his suggestions.

She slipped her long hair behind her ear and leaned forward, making the mark on her neck more visible. Ryan tensed when he saw it. Good. She remembered what Matt had told her.

"No, not really. Someone is trying to hurt me, Ryan. Before Agent Ross starts his questioning, I want you to know that Luke told me about the drugs. He confided that he wanted to get out. I'm worried that's what got him killed."

Her voice was calm and reassuring in a manner he wouldn't have thought possible, and he noticed Ryan soaked it in. Matt was amazed by her. How could she be so broken and battered and still so kind and calm? She wasn't projecting a victim mentality, and he admired that about her. She was a strong woman. He supposed she'd had to be. With that thought, his admiration for her turned to shame for what he'd done to her. Because of him, she'd had plenty of practice.

He saw Ryan's eyes shift as if wondering what he should say and what he shouldn't.

"Luke trusted me, Ryan. I hope you will, too."

Ryan sighed and raked a hand over his face. "The truth is, Miss Kendall, that Luke and I hadn't spoken much in the past few months. He pulled away from us. It's like he just changed. One day he was the same ole Luke and the next all he wanted to do was talk about God and go to church. He didn't want to party. He didn't want to go out. It's like he became a different person."

"What about the drugs?" Matt asked.

"You're not in trouble, Ryan. No one is interested in busting you. We only want to find out what happened to Luke. You were aware he was selling drugs to his friends?" Claire asked.

"Yes."

"Do you know how he got started doing it?"

"We met a guy at a party two years ago. We used to buy from him. He got Luke started selling."

Matt perked up at this information. "Did you know him? What's his name?"

"Steve Wilson. He was a senior at Morehead High School. If anyone knows who Luke's supplier is, it would be him. Luke never told me. We were always very competitive. I think he was worried I would try to take over his business. His parents are loaded, so he didn't need the money, but he enjoyed being the go-to guy. He thrived on the attention. I think it was because his parents, you know, didn't have a lot of time for him."

She thanked Ryan for being honest with her. Matt

asked him a few more questions, then Ryan stood to leave. He stopped in the doorway and turned to them, a solemn look on his face. "Luke was my best friend," he said. "I can't believe he's really gone. It wasn't supposed to be like this. It was just good fun. It's not like it's hard drugs."

Matt stood and faced him. He understood how Ryan was feeling. It was the same feelings he'd had after the accident. They'd only been having a good time and hadn't drunk much, but it had been enough to change both their lives that night. "Sometimes things aren't as black-and-white as they may seem. When I went to school here, I had a car accident after a night of innocent drinking. I hurt someone I cared a lot about and I ruined both our lives. Trixie is a dangerous drug, Ryan. It may seem harmless, but it's not. Don't let it pull you down the way I let alcohol do to me."

Ryan nodded, then left, and Matt closed the door behind him.

Claire was blushing when he turned around. "My life wasn't ruined."

His was and he wanted to tell her so. Living without her had changed him. Hurting her had changed him. The life he'd built wasn't bad, but it wasn't the one he'd wanted. But he knew saying that wouldn't do either of them any good.

Instead, he focused on the investigation. "Ryan gave us a name. Steve Wilson, formerly of Morehead High School. He should be easy enough to track down." He went to his laptop and used the DEA database to run down info on Steve Wilson.

"It looks like Wilson has been in prison for the past two years for possession with intent to distribute. According to DEA records, he's never given up his supplier."

He glanced up and saw Claire stand, her good hand rubbing at her hip. She moved slowly toward the window and looked out, her mind obviously sizing up the interview.

"You did good," he told her. "And you were right. Ryan opened up to you in a way I doubt he would have for me."

"I had to keep reminding myself that whoever killed Luke is also preying on these kids. They have no clue how dangerous this drug is. They think it's harmless. After you told me about the kids who have died, I Googled Trixie. It's bad news."

He nodded. "Don't worry, Claire. We'll find them."

"I'm still having trouble believing it's someone inside the school. You don't go into teaching because you want to make money. You have to care about these kids. I can't understand how someone can claim to care about them, then turn around and sell them something dangerous."

"We might not be looking for a teacher. It could be someone from the custodial staff, the lunch crew, secretaries, security, repairmen. There are a lot of people going in and out of this school. Principal Spencer gave me a list, and I'm following up on every one of them." He picked up the next file on his desk. "Next we're interviewing Melissa Bridges, Luke's girlfriend. I want to ask her about Luke's relationship with Ryan and see just how truthful he was being."

"You didn't believe Ryan?"

"It's not that I didn't believe him, but with Luke dead, his supplier will be looking for someone else to sell for him. It's possible Ryan might be their next recruit."

Melissa, Luke's on-again, off-again girlfriend, echoed much of what Ryan had said about Luke's pulling away from them. But she knew even less than Ryan about Luke's drug dealing. In fact, she claimed she never wanted to know.

"I liked Luke a lot," she said. "But we were never serious. We were just having a good time. At least, I thought we were. But that didn't mean I liked being cheated on."

"You think Luke was seeing another girl?"

"He was spending a lot of his time with someone, and it wasn't me."

Claire pressed for a name, but it was obvious Melissa didn't know. Though she had given them a lead that Luke had been possibly seeing someone else during the last few weeks of his life. Would this mystery girl know who killed him?

Claire knew Luke's salvation could have had a drastic change on his life and that could account for his pulling away from his friends. Unfortunately, he hadn't had time to help them understand his conversion before he'd been killed.

Ryan had said Luke craved the attention selling drugs got him, and it saddened her to think about that. Luke's parents were both professionals, but she knew they'd had little time to devote to their son. She understood Luke's need to find attention elsewhere.

She and Luke had come from the same kind of environment. In her home growing up, attention was at a premium. Her parents had been cold and distant, and she'd grown up feeling lonely and alone. Somehow she'd assumed that was what family was supposed to be...until she'd met the Ross family. Matt's family was so different from her own. They were warm and lovingly caring and had invited her to attend church with them. Had it not been for Matt and his family, she could have gone down the same path as Luke, or shut down altogether.

By the time Matt finished asking questions of the students, it was past school hours. She was glad to be able to help him with the interviews, but she missed her classroom and teaching. Principal Spencer had called in a sub for her for today, but she was ready to get back to it and soon.

Matt took a call from his DEA supervisor. While she waited, Claire realized she needed a textbook from her makeshift classroom. She wanted to have it to work out lesson plans tonight when she was certain sleep wouldn't come. She tried to get Matt's attention, motioning that she was going to run out to retrieve it, but he didn't seem to notice and she didn't want to disturb his phone call. Besides, she wouldn't be but a minute. The auditorium wasn't that far.

She walked the few doors down the hall, then noticed the crime scene tape had been pulled off the door of the lab. She heard raised voices coming from inside. Peering through the window on the door, she saw her fellow chemistry teacher Daryl Brown having a heated conversation with Ryan Summerhold. She was about to enter to ask them why they were there when Ryan's words stopped her cold.

"I did a job for you," she overheard him say. "I deserve to get paid what you promised me."

"All you did was make more trouble for me," Brown insisted. "I should have known better than to leave something so important up to a child."

"I'm not a child," Ryan told him, bitterness and anger coloring his tone, "and I can finish the job."

A sudden image of Luke lying dead in her classroom flashed through her mind and Claire removed her hand from the knob and backed away. Matt's words returned to her that Luke's supplier would be looking to recruit someone else. Had that already happened? And what could be the job Ryan felt he deserved to be paid for? Had Daryl paid Ryan to murder Luke? She shook her head. No, Ryan had said he could get the job done. That implied whatever Daryl had hired him to do was unfinished.

She turned to leave but tripped over the janitor's mop and bucket. The mop clattered to the floor.

"What was that?" Daryl demanded.

Claire heard footsteps approaching the door, but she couldn't move fast enough. The door swung open and both teacher and student stared at her on the floor.

"Miss Kendall? What happened?"

She decided her only option was to just pretend she hadn't overheard their conversation. "I was just walking by, but I tripped over the janitor's mop."

Daryl glanced up and down the hall, then reached to help her to her feet. "Why does he insist on leaving his equipment lying around? It's becoming a hazard. I plan to mention this incident to Principal Spencer. I suggest you do the same." He turned to Ryan. "We'll discuss this later."

The boy yanked up his backpack and stomped out of the room.

"Trouble?" Claire asked, referring to Ryan.

He waved it away. "Nothing I can't handle." He stepped back into the lab. "I was just looking for some microscope slides in the supply cabinet."

"Aren't you worried about contaminating the crime scene?"

He didn't seem to care. "The police have come and gone and already collected their evidence. Besides, classes must go on."

She nodded. "I believe there's a new box of slides on the top shelf to the right."

He made a show of looking at the cabinet, then nodded. "Yes, here they are." He pulled out the box and showed it to Claire. "Thank you. Well, I'll be going now. I have a pop quiz to prepare for my students tomorrow." He started to walk out, then turned back. "I should have told you sooner how sorry I am about what happened with Luke. I guess I didn't realize you two were so close."

"Thank you," Claire said, her mind still replaying the conversation she'd overheard. She didn't want to believe that a teacher would be the one behind the drugs in the school, but she knew someone was. And Matt had told her the drugs had to be mixed and packaged. Who better to do so than a person trained in chemistry?

She hurried from the room to fill Matt in, certain that what she'd witnessed between Mr. Brown and Ryan was suspicious and worth investigating.

* * *

Matt's heart dropped when he ended his call and saw Claire was gone. How could he protect her if she insisted on wandering off? His initial panic turned to agitation when he saw her in the hall in front of the lab.

"Claire, I thought we agreed it was safer for you to stay with me."

"I know. I'm sorry. I wanted to retrieve a textbook I needed. I thought I could do it quickly before you got off the phone, but I got distracted when I heard someone inside the lab." She relayed the conversation she'd overheard between Daryl and Ryan. "It's odd, don't you think?"

His interest was piqued. He pulled his laptop from his bag and scrolled through his files.

"I've been running background checks on all school faculty. His just came back today. It says here he teaches Advanced Placement chemistry."

"Yes, that's right. And Ryan is in my chemistry class, so he's definitely not one of Daryl's students. He's barely passing chemistry, but I've heard he's developed a skill for rebuilding engines."

Matt scrolled through the personnel file on Brown. "It looks like he worked for Mortan Pharmaceuticals for six years as a drug developer before coming to Lakeshore."

"I knew he worked in the private sector. He was one of those people the schools have been anxious to recruit, especially for science and mathematics."

"Mortan Pharmaceuticals? Where have I heard that name before?" He searched through his files again. "That's the same company Paul Thompson works for."

"Daryl and Luke's father were coworkers? If his father was friends with Daryl Brown, wouldn't he have pushed for Luke to get his old friend as a teacher?"

"Who said they were friends? Maybe Brown recruited Luke to get back at his father. We need to find out why Brown left Mortan Pharmaceuticals and how close he and Luke's father really are."

They had stopped walking in front of the wall of fame, a place near the office where framed photos of graduating classes were displayed. The school had class photos dating back thirty years, and they took up a large wall. Matt scanned the images, narrowing in on their graduation year, then on the faces until he found theirs. Their group picture had been taken two weeks before the wreck. In it, Matt's arms were around Claire and their big smiles spoke of happier days.

"Were we really that young and naive once?" he asked, thinking of how rosy the future had seemed to him back then. They'd made plans to marry and spend their lives together, and even now he knew it would have been amazing to be married to Claire. She had grown from a beautiful young girl into a beautiful and caring woman.

"I guess we were. It seems like a lifetime ago."

Her blue eyes gazed into his soul and he felt that old spark of electricity. He knew Claire felt it, too. He reached out and caressed her arm, and his heart kicked into high gear when he felt her shiver at his touch. He moved closer to her, ignoring every common-sense instinct he had to back away. Claire would never forgive him for leaving her no matter how great the attraction between them remained.

His phone rang, ending the debate with himself.

He backed away from her and glanced at the screen. "It's one of the security guys." He answered, then listened as the caller explained they'd found something he needed to see. "I'm on my way," Matt responded, then hung up.

"What is it?"

"There's something I need to check out on the back side of the parking lot."

Claire followed behind him as he headed toward where a group of students had gathered along with one of the security officers. "What happened?" he demanded, his adrenaline pumping and his fear of losing another student intensifying.

Several of them pointed toward the ground and Matt saw they were motioning to a storm drain. He wondered if perhaps they had seen a snake, but that suspicion was quickly dispelled. Something silver and shiny grabbed his attention farther down inside the drain. He couldn't see it fully but it looked like a knife. Could this be the one used to kill Luke? The assailant could have tossed it as he ran away.

Not wanting to disrupt any fingerprints that might be on the knife, he used a handkerchief and reached for the handle. A collective gasp and rush of chatter lit through the crowd as he pulled out the knife—a simple, silver cooking knife that looked to be from a kitchen set. It still had congealed blood on the blade. That would have to be tested for verification, but Matt was sure they'd just found the murder weapon.

FIVE

It was after dark before the police had finished processing the scene where the knife was found. Matt had wanted to stick around to make certain all evidence was collected properly and to help with the interviews of the students who'd found it. He'd kept Claire close by him at all times.

Afterward, they stopped by a drive-through burger joint before heading back to the house. Claire was surprised to see it dark.

"Dad texted me earlier and said they and Alisa were going out to dinner with Alisa's fiancé and future in-laws, so I guess we have the house to ourselves for a while."

Truthfully, she was glad to have a few hours of peace and quiet. She slipped her feet beneath her and curled up on the couch while Matt unloaded the bags of food.

Claire only picked at her burger and fries, her appetite nonexistent. She knew she needed to eat something, but she just couldn't bring herself to want it. Nothing in her life was going as planned and she was tired of not knowing whom she could or couldn't trust.

"I know it's disheartening," Matt told her, "but we'll figure this out. We'll find out who is behind all of this and we'll bring them to justice."

She nodded absentmindedly, which seemed to bother him.

"You can count on me, Claire. You know that, don't you?"

She was so tired she nearly assured him without thinking, but she stopped herself. Despite the ever-increasing attraction between them, she really wasn't sure she could put her faith in this man who'd already let her down before.

His expression tightened at her hesitation. "I know I've let you down in the past," he told her, "but I was just a kid back then. A dumb, frightened kid. I'm not that kid anymore and I'm not going anywhere as long as this threat is hanging over you." His eyes pleaded with her to understand. "You can depend on me. I want you to know that."

She wanted to believe him, and a part of her truly did. He was still the man she'd loved and trusted all those years ago, but her mind kept reminding her of the way her heart had been broken the last time she'd depended on him. "I want to trust you, Matt. I do. I just… I'm just so scared."

"I won't let anything happen to you."

He thought she meant she was frightened of who-ever was after her, and she was, but she was also scared of being betrayed again. She was scared of putting her trust in Matt and being disappointed. She might still be harboring unhealthy feelings for him, but she hadn't forgotten the heartache he'd inflicted upon her. In the end, she knew there was only one she could truly trust, and that was God. He would protect her and watch over her. He would see her through this nightmare.

"You're no longer the boy I used to know, but I don't know the man you've become. I honestly don't know if I can trust you or not. I want to. I need to, but I just don't know if I do yet."

He lowered his eyes, an injured expression on his face.

She reached out and touched his cheek, running her hand along the edge of his chin. His skin wasn't as smooth as she remembered and sadness had permeated his eyes. They'd both been through so many trials in the years that separated them and her heart ached for all the wasted time. But she couldn't focus on the past. She had to keep her eyes on the present, and for this moment in time, God had placed Matt Ross back in her life.

"But above all else, I'm a woman of faith and God has brought you back into my life at just the moment I needed someone, so I will try to trust you, Matt."

He gave her a halfhearted smile and kissed her hand still pressed to his face. "I won't let you down."

Claire turned in early, but Matt stayed up and continued going through the background checks.

He focused his attention specifically on Daryl Brown. Searching through DMV records, he discovered Brown had applied for a tag a few months ago for a black Chevy truck with a description that matched the one that had tried to run down Claire in the parking lot. His financials also raised red flags for Matt.

His bank account boasted more money than a school teacher should have on hand. Could it be drug money?

He closed the computer and rubbed his face, Claire's words echoing through his brain. He tried not to think about her hesitation when he'd said she could trust him. She didn't trust him and that was a problem he didn't know how to undo. He couldn't go back in time and change the way he'd behaved. If he could have, he would have done it a hundred times over the past years.

She believed God had sent him to be her protector. He was thankful for her faith, but how could he be when he didn't want to see God's hand in this? He wasn't on good terms with God. Too much had happened, yet he couldn't deny the urge inside him to pray for her safety. He wished he could trust God to watch out for her, to keep her safe, the way she trusted God. He longed for that assurance, that he was a part of God's plan and God was on his side. But his anger was too great. He'd been let down too many times.

He put his face in his hands as reality hit him as it always did. He'd been the good Christian boy and Claire had been hurt. He'd tried to be a good soldier and his team had been ambushed. He'd tried to be the best agent he could be and Luke had been murdered. It seemed no matter what he did on his own, bad things happened.

But how could he trust a God who'd already let him down multiple times, to keep Claire safe?

"Where are we going?" Claire asked as Matt took a turn away from the school the next morning.

"I want to check something out. I was running Daryl Brown's DMV records last night and found a black pickup registered to him."

She sucked in a breath. "Like the one that tried to run me down?"

"Exactly. I've been scanning the school parking lot for the truck ever since it tried to run you down. I haven't seen it on campus, so I thought we would drive by his house and see if he's keeping it there."

"You think Daryl is the one behind all this?"

"I can't say for sure yet, but his financials raised some doubts, as well. I plan to ask him some in-depth questions first thing today."

Even after all these years, the names of streets and locations came rushing back to him. He'd driven many of these roads for years. He stopped in front of an average-looking house on a tree-lined street. The number on the mailbox told him this was Brown's residence.

Claire leaned over and looked at the house. "It doesn't look like a drug dealer's home. I thought it would be bigger, grander."

He had to agree. "I don't see the truck."

"It might be in the garage."

As if on cue, the garage door opened and a car backed out. It wasn't the truck they were searching for but a maroon sedan. Brown was behind the wheel. As the car exited the garage, Matt saw no other vehicles inside. Brown noticed them, too, as he drove by, obviously on his way to work at the school.

Matt didn't flinch as Brown flashed them a curious glance. "He's driving a rental," he said as the car passed. "I saw the charge on his credit card statement."

"Then where is the truck he owns?"

"That's one question I intend on asking him." He put the car in gear and headed for the school.

As they pulled into the school lot, Matt did another scan of the vehicles, looking for the truck in question. Still not finding it, he parked and they got out.

"Stay close to me today, but I don't want you in the room when I interview Brown."

As they walked through the courtyard, Claire heard someone call to her. Jessica Alvarez approached, her long hair covering her face and her eyes darting nervously around as if always on alert for someone watching. "Miss Kendall, can I talk to you?"

She knew it wasn't a good time and almost told Jessica so. Matt wanted to get inside and question Daryl, but Claire couldn't ignore a student in need. She flashed Matt a give-me-a-second look and he stepped away, allowing them privacy while still remaining close by.

Claire sat down on a bench and motioned for the girl to do the same. "What's going on, Jessica?"

Jessica continued looking around anxiously. "I have to tell you something, but I'm scared. It's about Luke."

Claire's heart kicked a beat faster. Was it possible they were closer friends than Claire had originally thought? Melissa had stated she thought Luke was seeing another girl. If that were true, was it Jessica? "What is it?"

The girl bit her lip and fidgeted. She was on the cusp of spilling her secret and Claire had to force herself not to push her. She made her voice remain calm and placed a steadying hand on Jessica's arm. "Did Luke tell you who his supplier was?"

She shook her head. "No, he didn't. He never told me that."

"Then what is it?"

She took a deep breath and opened her mouth. "I saw—" She cut off abruptly and her eyes widened.

Claire squeezed the girl's fingers. "What did you see?"

She lowered her head and let her long hair cover her face. "Never mind. I have to go," she said, then jumped up and rushed away.

That was twice Jessica had tried to open up to Claire and both times something had stopped her. She saw in Jessica's face the fear that the entire student body carried. A student, one of them, was dead and now no one felt safe. Claire looked at Matt, who was scanning the courtyard. He was determined and persistent. He was their hope…her only hope.

She spotted Principal Spencer heading their way along with Preston and two uniformed officers a few steps behind him.

"Claire, Agent Ross, I was just coming to find you. Detective Ware was looking for you in the security office," Principal Spencer stated.

Matt immediately tensed. "We just arrived. What's happening?" he asked Preston. "Is there a break in the case?"

"There has been. Forensics came back on the knife. It was Luke's blood on the blade and—" Preston's steely eyes bored into Claire's "—your fingerprints on the handle."

Her heart sank. That couldn't have happened.

She'd never touched the murder weapon. She hadn't even seen the murder weapon.

She shook her head frantically. "No, that's not possible. It has to be a mistake."

"It's no mistake," Preston stated. "Your fingerprints are on file from when you applied for a teaching certificate. The match is indisputable. A team is already performing a search of your house. I'm sorry, Claire, I have no choice but to arrest you for the murder of Luke Thompson."

He pulled out his handcuffs and Claire moved back, running into Matt's solid frame. He stepped between her and Preston. "You don't honestly think Claire killed him, do you?"

"It doesn't matter what I think. The DA has seen the evidence. He wants her taken into custody and booked for murder."

"No, no!" Principal Spencer stepped forward. "This has to be a mistake. Claire would never harm a student."

"I'm sorry, Claire. I'm only doing my job."

She wasn't comforted one bit by his plea for understanding. She felt violated, exposed. At this very moment, strangers were pawing through her belongings looking for evidence to link her to Luke's murder. They shouldn't find anything because it didn't exist, but that thought didn't help. Not when they were also claiming her fingerprints were on the knife that was used to kill Luke.

Matt turned to her. "Think, Claire. When you entered the classroom and saw Luke on the floor, was the knife there? Did you pick it up?" She felt the anxiousness pouring off him. He was scared, scared of what this turn of events might mean.

"No. I didn't see any knife. I never saw a knife. Preston, you know me. You know I would never kill anyone. And I would never harm a student. I'm being set up."

"How do you explain that someone is after her if she's the one who killed Luke?" Matt demanded.

"Maybe she has an accomplice who wants to shut her up. Or maybe she made it all up and no one is really after her. She could be faking all of this to throw us off her scent. No one really knows what happened in that classroom except for Claire."

"I was in that classroom. I saw a man run out. Besides, she didn't shoot up her own house or drive the truck that nearly ran her down, did she? She didn't fake those incidents."

Preston reached around Matt and grabbed her arm. He slapped on the handcuffs, the metal digging hard into her wrists as they snapped shut. He recited the Miranda rights to her as he walked her toward his car. Opening the back door of his cruiser, he asked her, "Do you understand these rights as I've explained them to you, Claire?"

She nodded, then turned back for one last look at Matt, still standing in shock, before she allowed Preston to push her into the backseat and close the door.

It seemed everything about her life was falling apart, and now she was under arrest for Luke's murder. Could things get any worse?

"Don't worry, Claire," she heard Matt call after her. "We'll get this all straightened out."

She turned back to look at Matt, who stood at the curb watching the cruiser pull away.

As he drove to the police station, Matt was still trying to recapture the breath that had left him at the sight of Claire being taken away in handcuffs.

His mind wanted to refuse to accept this new information. Not Claire. Not his Claire. But he had to admit that Preston was right. Ten years could change a person. He was living proof of that. But how could Claire have changed that much? Was it possible she was behind Luke's drug involvement? Was she responsible for his death? Had she indeed killed him?

No!

People didn't change that much. And there had been a man in that classroom that day Luke was killed.

He waited at the jail until he could see her, then watched as she entered the interview room where he'd arranged to speak privately with her. She looked small and vulnerable, but her big blue eyes widened hopefully when she saw him.

He pulled her tightly into an embrace.

"How are you holding up?" he asked.

"I'm okay," she assured him, then her chin quivered. "I'm scared. I had nothing to do with Luke's death."

"I know and I'm going to prove it."

"What happens now?"

"You'll have a preliminary hearing tomorrow morning and the judge will set bond."

She nodded. "Then I can get out of here?"

"Yes." His heart ached at the thought of her being inside this place for even one night. He'd taken for granted that he'd be able to see her and talk to her.

"I promise you, Claire, I will find out who is behind this. I won't give up on you."

He thought he saw a momentary flash of concern in her face—like the one from the night before—then she smiled again. "Thank you."

But that momentary flash bothered him as he left the jail. He'd promised not to give up on her and she'd had a moment of doubt. Could he blame her? Hadn't he already left her once before when she needed him? He grimaced at the memory. Leaving Claire was one of his biggest regrets. He'd made excuses throughout the years, reminding himself that he'd only been a boy then and hadn't been prepared for the responsibility he shouldered. But that's all it was—excuses. He'd allowed his own guilt and shame to rule his life. But he was no longer a boy. He was a man now and he was used to taking on heavy burdens. It was time to face up to his own.

He owed Claire everything. But it was more than a guilty conscience that was driving him now. He believed in her and he couldn't—he wouldn't—allow her to take the fall for someone else. She had too good a heart to kill anyone in cold blood, much less one of her students. He'd spent the past ten years of his life learning to read people, and even if he hadn't previously known her, he would know she was incapable of doing what the police were charging her with. And if Preston believed it, then he didn't know Claire as well as he thought he did.

Matt's phone rang and he saw it was Brad Harris, his supervisor, calling. He answered it, prepared to give him an update, but he spoke first.

"I just learned that an arrest has been made in the Luke Thompson murder?"

How had his supervisor learned of the arrest and its specifics so quickly? "They did arrest someone, but I don't believe she's connected."

"According to the report I've obtained, the locals are claiming the boy's death had nothing to do with the drug ring. He had no drugs in his system and his suspected killer was his teacher. I think you're searching in the wrong place. Your only lead is dead and we have no other avenues to explore."

Matt saw his support with the agency faltering. "Sir, I disagree with the local police findings. I still believe following up on Luke's murder is the right way to continue."

"I don't think so, Matt. We need to focus our efforts elsewhere. I'll expect you back in the office tomorrow morning. We'll figure out a new course of action then."

Matt hung his head. He was being called off the investigation just when Claire needed him most. He hadn't been with the DEA long and he wasn't usually one to break the rules, but he also wasn't about to give up on Claire...not again.

"I have some vacation days saved up. I'd like to take them now if that's all right with you. I'm already back in my hometown, and my sister's wedding is coming up."

Brad sighed as if to let him know he wasn't fooling

anyone with his vacation request. "Okay, Matt. Then I'll see you back in the office next week." Before he disconnected, Brad said one more thing. "Be careful."

Matt assured him he would, then disconnected the call. He knew Claire had had nothing to do with Luke's death and he was still committed to finding out who did. But with one phone call from his supervisor, he'd just lost his backup at the agency.

He and Claire were on their own.

Why, God? Why?

Claire sat on the bed and leaned against the wall in her private cell. Why was this happening to her? First someone was trying to kill her and now she was being framed for murder? She didn't understand why someone, anyone, would want to do this to her.

Outside the bars that held her, she heard the sound of footfalls and shouts of curses and lewd comments. She didn't belong here and she was terrified of what her future now held.

She took a breath and tried to calm down, reminding herself that God was on her side. He would protect her even in this awful place and He would rescue her from this miscarriage of justice.

She thought of Matt and her revelation that God had sent him to her to protect her. She just had to hang on and have faith that he could clear her name. But doubts still crept into her mind. How could he shield her from a murder charge?

She closed her eyes and tried to breathe. All she could do was pray and answer their questions honestly, which she'd done. Yes, she had a set of knives like the one that had been identified as the murder weapon. She was certain a hundred other families had the same knife set in their kitchens. But she hadn't used hers to hurt anyone. In fact, she hadn't even used them to cook in weeks.

Someone spoke her name and she looked up to see Preston watching her through the bars. "Are you still mad at me?" he asked in a quiet voice.

She stood and approached the door. She'd had a lot of time to think and to realize that Preston was just doing his job. It didn't make her feel any better about the situation, but she couldn't fault him for it. "No, I'm not angry. But you have to know I had nothing to do with Luke's murder."

"I don't believe you're guilty, Claire, but the evidence against you is mounting. Forensics have identified your knife set matches the one they found with Luke's blood. Plus, your set is missing the chef's knife, the same type of knife used to kill Luke. And the DA is speculating that you sent that text to yourself from Luke's phone in order to give you an alibi. It was wiped clean of prints."

"I didn't. I'm telling the truth. You know me, Preston. You know I'm not capable of that kind of deceit."

He placed his hand over hers on the bar. "I know you're innocent, Claire, but the truth is that you can't always trust that you truly know someone. Some people are capable of more deceit than you would ever believe."

She supposed that was true. Someone—probably someone she knew—was responsible for Luke's death and a drug ring operating in her school. "I pray Matt can find out who is doing this to me soon."

Preston jerked his hand away at her words. "I don't understand why you're so dependent on a man who let you down when you needed him. I'm here for you, too, Claire. I'm working this case just as hard trying to find out who is setting you up."

"I know you are, Preston, and I'm thankful for you. You're a good friend."

"Besides, you may have no choice but to depend on me after today. The DEA has surrendered this case to Lakeshore PD. They're no longer involved."

"What?"

"The chief wasn't thrilled with them investigating in Lakeshore. He spoke to Matt's supervisor this morning and he's calling off Matt's investigation. He's probably packing his bags to leave town right now."

Claire's heart sank at this new revelation. Was Matt going to leave her again when she was counting on him for help?

Preston must have seen her agitation because he covered her hand with his once more. "I'm here, Claire. I'm not going anywhere, and I promise you I will find out who is trying to pin Luke's murder on you. I won't leave you. I will never leave you."

She tried to find comfort in Preston's words, but all she could focus on for the rest of the afternoon was the idea that Matt was being called off the investigation. Would he leave her? Would he drop the search for Luke's killer and leave her alone and in prison, taking the fall for something she didn't do?

She didn't want to believe it. But Preston had planted a seed of doubt that she couldn't brush away because he was right when he said it wouldn't be the first time Matt Ross had let her down when she'd needed him most.

Matt returned to the school intent on completing what he'd wanted to do before Claire was arrested. Even without the backing of his DEA supervisor, he wasn't giving up on Claire. He was going to find out who killed Luke, who was behind the threats against Claire and who was responsible for the Trixie ring operating in Lakeshore High School.

He was pulling into the parking lot when he spotted the very truck he'd been searching for parked in the teachers' lot. He slammed on his brakes and jumped out to examine the truck. It had the same tinted windows and a red sticker on the driver's-side windshield. Matt saw it was from a local golf club. He took out his phone and checked the vehicle registration number against the one he'd noted on Brown's registration. It matched.

He bent and looked at the front end where the truck that had tried to run down Claire had clipped the concrete barrier. This bumper had seen recent damage, confirming his suspicion that Brown was indeed the owner of the truck that had tried to run Claire down.

He returned to his own car and parked, then headed inside. It was time to confront Daryl Brown and get answers. Was he also responsible for setting up Claire for Luke's murder? But if he was, how had he done it? He rationalized Brown was a chemist. Surely he knew how to lift fingerprints and transfer them to the knife that had implicated Claire.

As he passed the office, Spencer rushed out and

walked with him. "How is Claire? I can't believe this is happening. Of course, I don't believe a word of it. Claire would never harm a student."

"She'll be better once I can prove she's being set up."

"What can I do?"

"Where's Daryl Brown?"

"In his classroom. Why?"

"He's about to need a substitute to finish teaching his class."

"Of course. I'll arrange to have someone go there right now." He rushed off and Matt headed for the science hallway and paced in front of Brown's door. He wanted nothing more than to burst in and drag Brown out, but he held back that impulse. He didn't need to traumatize these students any more than they already were. He would wait for Spencer to arrive with the sub.

The principal showed up a few minutes later with another teacher in tow. "This is Mrs. Wright. She has a free period right now."

"I'm glad to help," she stated. "I can't believe it about Claire. It just doesn't seem right. She's so sweet. She would never hurt anyone."

Matt was glad Claire had the support of her fellow teachers and her principal. He briefly wondered if they would feel the same about Brown if it turned out he was the killer. He wouldn't have to wait long to find out the answer.

Spencer opened the door and peeked inside, asking Brown if he could step into the hall for a moment.

"What's going on?" Brown demanded when he joined them.

"Agent Ross needs to ask you some questions," Principal Spencer stated. "They can't wait. Mrs. Wright will take over your class for now."

Anger and bitterness flashed through Brown's expression, then he gave Mrs. Wright the book he had in his hand. "There are copies of a pop quiz I was planning to give tomorrow in the top drawer of my desk. You might as well go ahead and give it, then have them read the next chapter for homework."

She took the book and nodded, then stepped into the classroom and closed the door.

"I'll be in my office if anyone needs me," Principal Spencer said, then walked off down the hall.

Brown looked at Matt. "What is this about?"

"I have a few questions about your truck," Matt told him, then walked outside to the parking lot.

"Is this your vehicle?" he asked, motioning to the black truck.

"Yes, it is. Why do you ask?"

Matt pointed toward the bumper. "Looks like you had an accident here."

Brown glanced at the bumper, then shook his head and sighed disgustedly. "Unbelievable."

"Maybe you heard about a truck trying to run down Claire Kendall several days ago. The vehicle that tried to run her down looked a lot like this one."

"Now wait just a minute," Brown demanded. "I had nothing to do with that. I haven't even had my truck for over a week. It's been at the mechanic's. I only just got the keys back today. You should know that since you saw me leaving my house in a rental car."

"Who's your mechanic?"

"I let a student do some work on the engine, Ryan Summerhold."

The same kid Claire had overheard Brown arguing with over money. Was it possible it was simply a discussion about the cost of repairs?

"So Ryan had the truck the day Claire was nearly run over?"

"Yes. I gave it to him last Friday. He said it would be ready by Monday, but then he kept putting me off. Finally, I'd had enough. I demanded he return it."

Was that the argument Claire had overheard? So Ryan was involved. Matt was sorry to hear that, and he knew Claire would be disappointed that the boy had stepped so easily into Luke's shoes.

But even if Ryan had been the one driving the truck, it didn't mean he wasn't working for Brown. "I know about your past work at Mortan Pharmaceuticals. You went from a six-figure annual income to a teacher's salary. That must have been quite a downfall. Why don't you tell me what happened?"

Daryl Brown grew defensive. "Why is my occupation any of your concern?"

"Because I'm here to ferret out whoever is behind this drug ring and right now you're looking pretty good for it, Daryl. You made your money for six years developing new drugs and now you're stuck in a school dealing with teenagers. Your truck was used to try to run down Claire, and you were overheard having an argument with Ryan Summerhold, the same boy you're saying had possession of your vehicle at the time of the incident. Now, maybe you want to answer my questions before I haul you to the police station for a much more detailed discussion."

Brown's eyes widened on hearing that he was considered a suspect. He rushed to answer Matt's accusations. "I had what my doctors called an emotional breakdown. I buckled under the pressure to always have to come up with the newest moneymaking drugs. Mortan poured millions into developing and selling new drugs, but it's a cutthroat world. Sure, the money is good, but the stress made me an old man before I was forty. I still have a substantial savings and my house is paid for, so this position at Lakeshore was a good fit for me. The school wanted someone with a solid background in professional science to complement their new science program, while I get to share my wisdom and have summers off to travel."

"And the argument between you and Ryan?"

He laughed, then shook his head. "As I said, I enlisted Ryan to do some mechanic work on my truck. Academically, he's not a great student, but the boy is a genius with mechanics. I paid him $1,500 for a new engine that he said needed to be replaced." He shrugged. "It's cheaper than buying a new car. But when I wanted my truck back, he tried to claim it needed additional repairs. I didn't believe him. Now I suppose I know why he didn't want to return my vehicle. He used it to commit a crime."

"So you have no involvement in the drug ring that's operating out of Lakeshore High?"

"Look, Agent Ross, I might have had some problems, but I went into pharmaceutical research because I wanted to help people. Doping up teenagers isn't what I would consider a valuable contribution to society. Not only is it morally reprehensible, but as I stated, I don't need the money, so there's really no reason for me to waste my time on that kind of junk chemistry."

Brown's denial seemed genuine and he'd logically explained his change in careers, his hefty bank account and the use of his vehicle in the attack on Claire. Matt's gut was telling him he wasn't the supplier. He would keep Brown on his radar, but he no longer believed Brown was the drug supplier.

However, what Brown had just told him had strengthened the case against Ryan Summerhold, throwing more light on the boy's involvement in the affair.

SIX

Before the wreck on prom night, Matt had been active in church and a strong believer in God. However, since that night, his faith had taken a backseat to grief and guilt. But now, something had changed in his life again.

He opened the nightstand drawer in his boyhood bedroom and pulled out his old Bible. He'd left it behind when he'd joined the army, angry and bitter at God for the wreck and for losing Claire. He'd remained angry at God for so long that it had simply become a part of his life to keep Him at arm's length.

But tonight, he took out his Bible and walked into the backyard. If he ever hoped to have a future with Claire—which was more and more on his mind these days—when this was all over and she was out of danger and cleared of this outrageous murder charge, he knew he had to also fix his relationship with God. Claire had said herself she was a woman of faith and she would never want someone who hadn't spoken to the Lord in years.

He opened to Genesis and turned to the story of Joseph. Ever since Claire had mentioned studying that, Matt had felt a connection. He remembered the story from his childhood, but he read it now with fresh eyes.

Like Joseph, who had been betrayed by his brothers, Matt knew the sting of betrayal. He and his ranger squad had been betrayed by a translator embedded with them who had led them straight into an ambush. He knew that topsy-turvy feeling of watching his life spin out of control, out of any ordered way he'd thought it would go. Joseph surely had had plans for his future that didn't include being sold into slavery and spending years in prison and servitude. Matt could relate. After the ambush of his ranger squad, he'd been distraught. He'd expected to remain a ranger for many more years, but the injury he'd sustained in the attack had left him in constant pain. He'd held on for several months, even completing another mission with the rangers, but his heart was no longer in it. Matt reminded himself now that God had used Joseph's tragedy for good. He'd had a plan for Joseph's life, and He had a plan for Matt's.

He would never have thought God's plan would bring him back into contact with Claire, but how else could he account for being in the same school at the same time just when she needed him?

He rubbed his face. He tried so hard to keep it together, to not allow himself to fall apart under the pressure, but it was hard. He'd lost so much already. Now Claire was in trouble. And once again he was pounding his fists trying to make things happen.

He heard the back door open and his father joined him on the patio, a fresh cup of coffee in his hand. "You're up late."

Matt nodded. "Just doing some thinking."

He motioned toward the Bible on the table. "Good to see you have that open again. Anything you want to talk about?"

Matt told him the truth. "I've spent my entire army career making sure I kept my nose clean and my reputation was spotless."

"Nothing wrong with that."

"It's all been a lie, Dad. My reputation is anything but spotless. No matter how far I ran from the consequences of that wreck, it was never far enough to make me forget. I suppose I never realized until recently what you must have had to go through to keep them from pressing charges against me. I could never have joined the army with a DUI hanging over my head. You covered for me."

His father shrugged. "I did what any parent would do in that situation. I begged Claire's parents and the DA for leniency."

"You did? Why did you do that?"

"Because I'm your father. It's a parent's job to look out for their kids."

"Sometimes it's better for a kid to suffer the consequences of their actions."

"Sometimes. But then you were always harder on yourself than a normal kid, and sometimes there's more than enough consequences to deal with without piling on. We all saw that, even the Kendalls."

Matt realized he wasn't any different from any of those kids Claire taught now. He'd been spoiled and entitled. He'd been one of them. "They could have ruined me."

"But they didn't. You turned out to be a fine young man."

"I've been running from that night my whole life. It defines me."

"No, son. Who you are as a man defines you. Your relationship with the Lord is what truly defines you."

"My relationship with God has been nonexistent for years. Sometimes I wonder if He's forgotten about me."

"He hasn't. He can't, any more than your mother or I could forget about you."

"I've done so many things I regret, Dad. My whole life has been one mistake after the next and so many people have been hurt. Do you think Claire can ever truly forgive me for what I've put her through?"

His dad smiled. "I think Claire has never been the type of person to hold grudges. She's a fine young woman. We've always thought so. Besides, if she couldn't forgive you, I doubt she'd be putting such trust in you now."

"I've been called off the investigation. My supervisor believes it's a dead end. He wants me to find other leads."

His father nodded his head. "I guess that means you'll be leaving soon?"

"No. I can't believe how much I still care for her even after all these years. When I saw her being arrested, it felt like my heart was being cut out. I know it's probably too late for us to be together. Too much has happened between us. But I can't walk away from her again. Not while she's in danger."

"Well, son, I don't think it's ever too late when love is involved. But if you're working without your DEA resources, you'll need backup. I'm not as young as I used to be and we still have all this wedding stuff to deal with, but I'll do whatever I can to help you."

Matt smiled. He'd expected nothing less than his father's offer of help, but his family was already overwhelmed with the wedding. "I appreciate the offer, Dad, but I'm not alone. I have the rangers to back me up."

He would drop everything to aid one of his ranger brothers—and had when Josh had needed their help—but he hated asking for it for himself. But this wasn't about him. He let his mind drift back to ten years ago, to the good times before the car wreck. He and Claire had laughed together, studied together, served in the church youth group together. Even then her kindness and compassion had been evident in her everyday life. She wasn't capable of the kind of violence she was being accused of. She was innocent, and she was depending on him to prove it. He wouldn't let her down again.

He pulled his phone from his pocket and scrolled through his contacts until he found Garrett's number. When his friend answered, Matt got right to the point.

"I need your help."

Matt drove two hours to meet up with Garrett and Josh, two of his ranger buddies who had also left the army.

"I know it's a lot to ask," Matt said after spilling the details of his and Claire's predicament.

Josh dug through the files Matt had provided him. "So you believe whoever killed Luke is also behind the drug ring?"

"Yes, and the one setting up Claire. She did not kill anyone. Now I just need to prove it."

"Can I make a suggestion?" Garrett asked.

"What is it?"

"It seems to me you're too emotionally involved with this. Maybe you need someone else to take a fresh view. They might see something that you're missing."

Matt was a little uncomfortable having someone else realize his personal connection to the case. He'd always liked to keep his emotions in check during his time with the rangers. Emotion made you reckless and after the wreck he'd vowed to never be reckless again. Still, he would do whatever it took to protect Claire, even if that meant bowing to his ego.

"That's why I called the two of you."

"And we're glad to help," Garrett stated, "but I was thinking Elise might be a good person to ask, as well. She's an FBI-trained investigator."

Josh nodded. "That's not a bad idea. I can take her these files and let her look through them. Maybe she can see something you've missed."

Matt nodded. "I would appreciate that."

"No problem, brother. You know the rangers are always here for you."

Matt realized he owed his brothers a lot for how they'd come through for him. He owed them the truth about himself and about what had really happened ten years ago.

"There's something you should know about me and Claire. We were in love a long time ago."

"I take it that didn't end well?" Josh asked.

"That's an understatement. I've never told anyone

about this." He went on to tell them about the accident and how he'd abandoned Claire to join the army.

Garrett whistled when Matt finished his story. "Wow. I can't believe you've kept that secret for so long."

"It's my deepest regret. I hope this doesn't affect how you both see me."

They looked at each, then Josh responded, "Well, it does, Matt. Frankly, it makes you seem more—"

"Human," Garrett finished.

"Human," Josh agreed.

"So you don't think less of me now?"

"Of course we don't think less of you. You messed up. Who hasn't?"

"Yes, but my mess up cost someone I care about a great deal of pain."

"That doesn't make you special, Matt. It just makes you…" He looked at Garrett again as if he couldn't pinpoint the word he was searching for.

"Human," Garrett finished, smiling.

Josh nodded. "Exactly. Welcome to the human race."

Matt grinned at their lightheartedness. "Guys, I messed up here. I mean I really messed up. This one mistake has haunted me for ten years. Now I have an opportunity to redeem myself in Claire's eyes."

"You can't change the past. All you can do now is try to make her future better."

"And I intend to do just that," he told them.

Claire noticed Matt in the courtroom Friday morning when she was arraigned. He looked solid and so handsome, but his face showed weariness. He was there, though, and she was glad to see him. She hadn't had the opportunity yet to speak with him since Preston had told her about the DEA dropping their investigation. She was ashamed to admit she'd wondered if she would see him again.

Lloyd Wingate, her father's attorney, was there, too, and she was thankful for his presence. He addressed the court on her behalf, arguing for her release, and arranged to have her bail paid, knowing her father would reimburse him once he returned to town.

"We need to start preparing for a trial," Lloyd told her as Claire's personal items that had been collected when she was arrested were returned to her. "Our firm doesn't handle criminal defense cases, but since your father is one of my biggest clients and my friend, I'm going to personally contact a criminal defense lawyer on his behalf. He'll be in touch with you in the next few days to schedule a meeting to go over the case. I've also arranged to have your parents contacted on board their cruise ship. I'm certain this is not how they imagined spending their vacation, but I'm sure they would want to know."

Claire wondered if they would cut their trip short knowing that she was in trouble. Somehow she doubted it. Her father trusted Lloyd thoroughly, and if he was handling things, then her father would assume that Claire's case was in good hands. She could almost hear her father's reprimand that there was no need for them to come home early, since there was nothing they could do here anyway.

She wondered if other parents reacted the same way. Would the Ross family react that way had Matt been the one arrested? No. She knew emphatically they would drop whatever was going on in their lives to be by his side for emotional support even if there was nothing they could do to help the situation. It seemed to her that only her family was the oddity.

She'd always sensed something was different about her family, even if she never knew exactly what it was...until she'd met the Ross family with their close ties, in obvious contrast to her own.

She chided herself. Poor little rich girl. Mommy and Daddy didn't love her enough. She knew there were so many people with such worse problems in life than a lack of affection from their family. At least her parents were always willing to help her financially when she needed it, as she did now. Her father wouldn't hesitate to pay for a defense attorney for her.

Matt was waiting for her outside when Claire was finally released. He waved and gave her a slight smile that made her weak-kneed. It wasn't fair that he still had such a pull on her even after all these years.

She walked toward him, conscious of the discomfort in her hip after spending the night on the flimsy jailhouse mattress. Stress always brought out the stiffness in her joints. She hated for Matt to see her limp. It had to be the final nail in the coffin of their once amazing romance.

She held her head high as she moved. What did it matter if her limp was noticeable? Their relationship had been over for a very long time.

"Are you okay?" he asked, concern lining his face. He cupped her face in his hands and she longed to step right into his arms and let him assure her everything would be all right.

"I'm fine. What are you doing here?"

"I came to take you home."

She liked the way he referred to his family's house as her home. She'd always been comfortable there and that hadn't changed. Staying with the Rosses had kept her feeling safe and loved, but she supposed that would all change when Matt left again. "Preston told me about the DEA dropping the case." She lowered her head, not wanting him to see how his leaving upset her. "I suppose this means you'll be leaving town soon."

He lifted her chin with his finger until she locked eyes with him. "I'm not going anywhere, Claire." His eyes sparkled as he reassured her.

"But the case—"

"Doesn't matter to me as much as you do. I won't leave until I know you're safe and your name is cleared," he promised her. "A couple of my former ranger friends are going to help us figure out who is behind this. I won't let anything happen to you."

Her eyes filled with tears at his declaration. "I'm scared," she admitted. Scared of what was happening to her. Scared of how much she wanted to believe in him again. She hated herself for doubting him for even a moment. She wanted to trust him completely, unabashedly, but when she'd had the opportunity, she had to admit she'd failed him. Everyone deserved another chance and she wanted to give Matt that second chance.

He pulled her into his arms and she went willingly, happily, drawing her strength from his presence. And maybe they could even have a second chance at love, too.

* * *

They met Matt's friends at a truck stop diner that was open all night.

Matt headed toward a booth where two men and a woman sat. They stood to greet them. The woman— Matt introduced her as Elise—was a dark-haired beauty with a look that shouted professional even in her jeans and blouse. She was also sporting a big diamond on her ring finger. Next to her was Josh, who was tall, though not as tall as Matt. He was slim and lean with dark hair and bright blue eyes. Garrett, the second man, had a much younger-looking face and a mop of dirty-blond hair on his head that matched the goatee. He had a big smile and an easygoing manner.

"Garrett's a hacker," Matt said. "He can get into any system and find out pretty much anything he needs to know."

Garrett grinned and shook his head good-naturedly. "No one says hacker anymore. I prefer to be called an information broker." He smiled at Claire. "That's a little skill I learned before joining the army and it has served me well since reentering civilian life."

"It's nice to meet you," Elise said, extending her hand for Claire to shake. "I wish it were under better circumstances."

"It's nice to meet you all. Thank you for your help."

"The rangers are always here for one another," Josh told her. "Whenever, wherever."

"And even though I'm not officially a ranger, I'm always glad to help, too," Elise said.

Matt ushered her into one side of the booth and took the seat beside her while Josh and Elise sat on the opposite side. Garrett grabbed a chair, turned it around and sat at the end of the table.

As Matt recounted every detail of what they'd been going through, Claire shuddered at hearing it repeated aloud all at once. It seemed as if it had been a long time since Matt had walked back into her life, but in reality it had only been five days. Five days since she'd been lured to the school to find Luke dead... and now multiple failed attempts on her life.

Garrett grinned as Matt explained how Claire had used the sodium metal to escape the attack in the lab. "Clever girl," he said. "I like that. It shows determination." He nudged Matt. "Now I see why you fell so hard for her."

Matt stiffened at Garrett's words about falling for her. He glared at Garrett, then glanced at Claire with what she could only call a stricken look. "I—I never told him that I had fallen hard for you."

She tried to smile graciously, but her heart was breaking at the way he stumbled over his words, trying to assure everyone that he didn't have feelings for her. It was only another reminder that she wasn't the girl he used to know. Somehow his repeated insistence hurt more than the cord around her neck had.

"I have some papers in my car," Matt said. "Garrett, will you help me get them?"

Garrett nodded and they got up and walked out.

"Don't mind them," Josh told her. "Garrett is kind of known for sticking his foot in his mouth."

Elise leaned forward. "I've heard Matt's version of what happened. Now I'd like to hear yours." She led Claire through several of the attacks, asking probing questions.

"Now tell me about the incident in the lab. What happened exactly?"

Claire rubbed the raw area on her neck as she spoke, reliving each terrifying moment and realizing Matt had been in what she'd believed might be her last thoughts.

"What about his clothes? Was there anything unusual in his attire?"

She shook her head. "I don't remember. It all happened so fast.'

"You said you didn't see his face," Elise continued. "Did you see his eyes?"

"Yes. Through the holes in the mask."

"Can you describe them?"

"They were light-colored, maybe green or gray. I saw anger in them. They were glowing with white-hot rage. That's how I knew he wanted me dead and wasn't just trying to scare me." Fear rippled through her as she remembered the hatred she'd seen there, and she knew he would have taken satisfaction in killing her.

Claire rubbed her face, weariness spreading through her. Would they ever find out who was behind this mess?

Elise reached across the table and placed her hand over Claire's. "Don't worry. We'll figure this out. You're not alone in this."

Claire glanced at the empty seat where Matt had been and remembered his reaction to Garrett's words. Why then did she suddenly feel so alone?

✳ ✳ ✳

"Are you insane?" Matt demanded when he and Garrett were outside.

Garrett looked surprised by the outburst. "What did I do?"

"Saying I was falling hard for Claire right in front of her. How could you do that?"

"I didn't know it was a secret."

"It's not a secret because it's not true."

Garrett gave him a skeptical look, then grinned. "Yeah, it is. It's so obvious."

Was he that transparent with his affection for Claire that even Garrett could see it? Did that mean Claire could, as well? He raked a hand through his hair and decided to come clean with his friend. "Look, Claire and I were an item when we were kids, but that ended a long time ago and it ended badly. Claire's not interested in rekindling that spark."

"How do you know unless you try? You obviously care about her. I've never seen you this way before, Matt. That lady has poked some holes through your cool exterior."

He was known by the rangers and all who encountered him throughout his army career as levelheaded and emotionless. He'd left Claire when he was full of anger at her refusal to see him and guilt over the accident. He'd made the second biggest mistake of his life in leaving her, and he'd learned the hard way not to let emotion drive his actions. But Garrett didn't know that side of him.

"I told you what happened between Claire and me. I left her, Garrett. I ran away and that's something that cannot be forgiven. So, yes, I do care for her a lot, but we can never be anything more than friends."

Garrett had to understand that he and Claire could never have a future together, no matter how much he wanted one.

Elise had Matt and Claire walk them all back through each incident again as a separate event, examining the players and the evidence of each. They spread out the files and even moved to a bigger table to give them more room to work. Thankfully, the diner was nearly empty, so it wasn't an issue.

"There is a lot going on here," Elise stated, "but it looks to me to be two places to focus on, inside the school and outside the school. Inside we have an unknown, and by extension his possible recruit, Ryan."

Matt saw disappointment line Claire's expression, but she nodded. "Ryan did say he and Luke were also competitive. He believed Luke didn't tell him about his supplier because he might try to supplant him."

"And whoever Luke's supplier was, he'll need someone new to push his merchandise," Matt agreed.

"I'd focus on putting pressure on Ryan to give up his supplier," Elise continued. "His background doesn't suggest he's been in any real trouble before. He's probably in way over his head and doesn't even realize it. He's definitely your weak link."

"That's what I was thinking, too," Matt said.

"That could put the kid in danger," Garrett stated. "Whoever killed Luke probably wouldn't hesitate to kill him, too, if he thought he might talk."

"Also, I would dig further into Luke's life. Someone close to him knows what's going on. I know you spoke with some of his friends, but they all stated in their interviews that Luke had pulled away from them, that he'd become distant."

"That's right," Claire said. "He'd become a Christian. His friends didn't understand that."

"Even a new Christian needs someone to talk to, someone who understands him. Luke had to have been sharing what was going on in his life with someone else."

Claire looked at Matt. "Melissa did say she thought Luke was seeing another girl."

"But who?"

"Jessica Alvarez. She's tried several times to speak to me, but each time something has spooked her and she's rushed away before she could. I was going to suggest she speak with one of the counselors, but maybe there's more to her behavior than simple grief over a fellow student's loss. She does seem overly distraught by Luke's death."

"We never interviewed her because she wasn't on the list of Luke's close friends."

"No, they weren't friends. At least, I didn't think they were. They ran in different circles, but Luke was liked by so many people. It's possible they had a connection I knew nothing about."

"We need to speak to Jessica as soon as possible."

"Principal Spencer is another person you should be focusing on," Elise stated.

"Principal Spencer?" Claire exclaimed. "That's unlikely."

Elise continued despite her outburst. "He fits the description of the man who attacked you in height, weight and eye color according to his Tennessee driver's license. Plus, he's the one responsible for hiring the security at the school. I noticed in your notes, Matt, that you wrote the security team was markedly untrained, which made the high school an ideal location to peddle illegal drugs."

"That's true. The security at that school was terrible and it's seemingly been that way for some time. And Spencer is always hanging around asking questions about the investigation."

"He's the principal of a school where a known drug ring is operating. I'd say he has reason to question," Josh stated.

"True, but we should check into his financials to be sure nothing suspicious turns up just in case." They all nodded, but Claire was obviously still skeptical.

"Principal Spencer has been nothing but good to me. Besides, it couldn't have been him who attacked me in the lab. Wasn't he in the auditorium with you?" she asked Matt.

Matt thought back, trying to place where the principal had been. He had definitely been there up until Matt had stepped on stage and addressed the assembly. After that, when the arguments erupted, Matt couldn't recall seeing him. How easily could he have slipped away to try to strangle Claire when he saw her sneak out?

The crowd had definitely gotten unruly and Matt couldn't pinpoint exactly where Spencer had been during the commotion. Matt had given up on restoring any kind of order when he'd noticed Claire was gone. He shook his head. "I can't say for sure, but it would be a big risk for him to try to sneak away and attack you."

Elise continued to her next point. "We have to also consider Ryan's tip about Steve Wilson. Someone outside the school might be pulling the strings."

"I tracked Wilson down through his prison records," Matt said. "He's currently serving a ten-year stint in a Memphis prison. According to his records, he's been uncooperative with the police in giving up his supplier."

"Josh and I can take a drive down there to interview him," Garrett said, and Josh readily agreed.

Matt shook his head. "I can't ask you to do that."

"You didn't. We just volunteered. Don't worry, Matt. I haven't forgotten how to get information from a hostile informant."

"But if Ryan is involved as you suspect, that tip could be bogus," Josh stated.

"If it is, we'll find out," Garrett told them. As the meeting wore down and they all had areas to focus on, Matt took a moment to thank each one of them for their help.

Elise shook her head. "No thanks are necessary. You all were there for me when I needed help. Brooke and I wouldn't have made it out of that cabin alive if not for the rangers." Elise looked at Claire and explained. "Josh's niece was kidnapped by a human trafficking ring I was investigating. I found her and helped her escape but managed to get myself and another kidnapped girl trapped in a cabin with a madman. Josh, along with the rangers, rescued us."

"That's not exactly how it went," Josh stated. "She did a bit of tail kicking before we were able to get there." He leaned over and kissed her, and Matt thought he'd never seen Josh so happy.

He envied his brother that. Despite the fact that she was sitting right beside him, the only woman he'd ever loved was out of his reach. He remembered how frantic Josh had been when he thought he might have lost Elise for good. Matt and Colton had calmed him down, but Matt had secretly known just how he'd felt at that moment. It was the same horror he'd experienced the night of the accident after they'd wheeled Claire into the hospital and he hadn't known if she would survive her injuries, while he'd walked away with nothing but scratches. Josh had recovered the woman he loved, but Matt had not... not until he'd seen her standing over the dead body of Luke Thompson.

He knew what he'd told Garrett was true. There was no way Claire could ever forgive him for leaving her the way he did, but that didn't mean he didn't care about what happened to her. He would make sure she was safe before he walked out of her life again.

Claire was eager to speak with Jessica off school grounds. Maybe she could finally convince the girl to share what she'd been too frightened to say before. Matt pulled up at Jessica's home and cut the engine, and they walked together to the door. He rang the bell and the door was opened a moment later by Jessica's mother.

"Hi, Mrs. Alvarez, I'm Claire Kendall, one of Jessica's teachers. I was hoping we could have a word with her."

The woman folded her arms. "I know who you are. You're that teacher who murdered her student."

Matt quickly stepped in to defend her before she could defend herself.

"Claire did not kill him. She did all she could to help him. And the DEA is working with the local police to find out who is behind Luke's death."

"Then why did the police arrest her?"

"That was a mistake. She's innocent."

Claire was thankful he was here beside her and thankful for his quick defense. It felt good to have someone on her side. "I understand Jessica was close to Luke. We were hoping she might have some information that would be helpful to the investigation."

At the top of the stairs behind Mrs. Alvarez, Jessica appeared, stopping when she saw them at the door. "Miss Kendall, what are you doing here?"

Claire noticed the girl looked pale and frightened. "Jessica, we were hoping to talk to you about your relationship with Luke."

"No," Mrs. Alvarez interrupted. "I don't want you talking to my daughter. I don't even want you around her. In fact, I haven't even decided if she'll be returning to school."

"Mother, don't blame Miss Kendall. She had nothing to do with Luke's death."

"I don't care," her mother insisted. "I don't want you involved." She turned back to Matt and Claire. "I have to look out for my daughter." She shut the door as Jessica continued protesting.

Claire felt her heart fall. She'd been hoping Jessica might be a key to uncovering Luke's killer, and now they weren't even allowed to speak to her.

"What are we going to do now?" she asked.

He shrugged and she could feel the frustration

flowing off him. "It's not an official investigation anymore, so I can't compel her to answer questions."

They were nearly to the car when the front door opened and Jessica called to them and ran out to meet them. "I told my mom that I want to talk to you. She's worried about me, but she gave her okay."

Claire stepped forward. Mrs. Alvarez was standing at the door. She didn't look happy but she nodded her agreement to the interview.

"I want to tell you what I know."

"And what's that, Jessica?"

"I think I know who killed Luke."

SEVEN

Mrs. Alvarez paced the kitchen floor, her arms folded and her face drawn. Matt could see she was nervous about Jessica's involvement and he understood her apprehension. A boy was dead, and her child was too close to the situation. What Jessica knew about the murder might put her in danger.

Jessica looked frightened and picked at her cuticles nervously as she sat across from them at her kitchen table.

"Don't be afraid," Matt told her, and Claire was in awe of his gentle manner. He understood that Jessica had been through a difficult time and was frightened and he was doing all he could to reassure her. "Just tell us what you know."

"I was leaving school one afternoon and Luke and I were supposed to meet up. I went to meet him and I saw he was talking with Principal Spencer. I didn't think anything about it until I saw Principal Spencer grab Luke's arm. He looked angry and he was yelling. He said Luke would be sorry if he tried to double-cross him. He said he would kill him if he tried."

Claire sucked in a breath. Principal Spencer. No

wonder Jessica had been so frightened every time she'd seen him. "Did he see you, Jessica? Did he know you overheard that conversation?"

"I don't think so. I hid behind a corner and waited until he was gone. When I asked Luke what he was so mad about, he only shrugged and said it was no big deal. Luke was dead two days later."

Mrs. Alvarez gasped. "Principal Spencer? The principal of the school killed someone? That's it, Jessica. You're not going back there."

"I actually think that's a good idea," Matt said. "If Spencer is the killer and he even suspects you know about that conversation with Luke, you could be in danger."

"There are several families who haven't allowed their kids back to school yet. I don't think your absence would raise any flags," Claire told them.

Jessica's eyes widened. "But won't he go to jail?"

"We can't arrest him until we have more evidence to back up your statement. But don't worry. Now that I know where to focus my investigation, we'll find it." Matt gave her another reassuring look. "You did good, Jessica. You've been a big help, but you don't have to worry anymore. You're not in this alone."

Claire was impressed with the gentle manner Matt had with Jessica, but as he stood to place a call to Garrett, Claire could see the fear in both Jessica's and her mother's faces. The girl was taking a risk stepping out in faith, trusting that Matt and Claire could protect her and bring Luke's killer to justice. Claire realized she, too, needed to act on faith.

She reached for Jessica's hand. "I admire your courage, Jessica. Can I pray for you?"

She nodded, and after Mrs. Alvarez joined them, Claire lifted a prayer for Jessica's safety.

Matt phoned Garrett and related what Jessica had told him.

"Do you think you can get access to Spencer's financial records?" Matt asked.

Garrett chuckled in an arrogant manner. "Do I think I can get access? That's cute, Matt. Now ask me for something hard."

"I ran a preliminary record on all the teachers and staff, but his didn't raise any red flags. Now I want a more comprehensive check of his background. Right now, he's our only suspect."

"I'll phone if I find something."

He hung up with Garrett, then turned and saw Claire speaking low with Jessica and wondered if they were discussing the case. Then he saw Claire reach for Jessica's hand and bow her head, praying with the girl and her mother. He smiled, knowing she was picking up with Jessica where Luke had left off. He liked that.

Claire stood and hugged Jessica, then joined Matt as they walked to the car. "She's going to be okay."

"I'm getting background and financials on Spencer, but I think it's time to include Preston in this, as well. He'll want to speak with Jessica, too. What do you know about Principal Spencer?" he asked Claire. Spencer wasn't from Lakeshore, so Matt had never met him previously.

"He was hired by the school board two years ago from a school in Nashville. He's been a good principal, fair and efficient. Everyone likes him, the faculty and the students. I can't believe he could be involved in the murder of a student."

"Well, we don't know yet that he was. We need to find proof." He was glad to have another lead to investigate, with the Brown lead not panning out.

She shuddered and folded her arms over her chest. "I don't even know how to act around him now. What do I say? What do I do?"

"Nothing. You can't do anything that might alert Spencer that we suspect him. You have to continue on just like before."

"I'm not sure I can."

"Whatever you do, Claire, don't let on that we're investigating him. If he did kill Luke, he's likely already on edge, suspicious of everyone and everything uncovering his secret." He looked at her and saw this revelation was already affecting her. "Maybe it would be a good time to take a few days off. No one would blame you." Before she could protest, he continued. "I may have to go meet with Garrett and Josh again after they interview Wilson. I would feel better if you were with me, so I'd know you were safe."

She hesitated. Yes, it was a lame excuse, but it was obvious she needed a reason not to return to school and have to face Spencer.

"Fine," she said. "I'll take a few sick days."

She didn't have to phone the school about taking a few days off. As it turned out, Principal Spencer was waiting for them at the Ross house when they returned.

Matt tensed when he spotted Spencer on the front porch with his folks having tea and conversing. Claire found it difficult to believe that this man could be the one behind her attacks and Luke's death. He was caring and concerned about the students. He'd been a good principal and a good friend to her.

He stood as they approached and his easygoing manner she'd seen with the Rosses evaporated. His face grew solemn.

"Principal Spencer, what are you doing here?" she asked him.

"I came to speak with you, Claire. I'm afraid I have some news."

Her heart skipped a beat. Had another student been injured or killed? It broke her heart to think of the possibility.

"I wanted to be the one to tell you myself. I thought it would be better coming from me."

"What is it?" she pressed him. "Tell me."

"The school board had an emergency meeting. They've decided to place you on temporary suspension."

"What? They can't do that. I haven't done anything wrong."

"This isn't permanent. It's just until after the trial."

Assuming she was proven innocent. He didn't say the words. He didn't have to.

"This isn't right. I'll appeal this decision."

"You can try, but I will tell you there are a lot of parents who are lobbying for your termination. They're threatening to pull their kids out of school, and they make large donations to the political parties here in town."

"I had nothing to do with Luke's death." How many times did she have to proclaim her innocence?

"Of course I don't believe you had anything to do with that, but you did meet secretly with a student outside of school hours. You also knew and hid from his parents, the school and the police the knowledge that Luke was selling drugs. Some of the parents feel that if they can't trust you to tell them when their child is in trouble, then they don't want you around their child."

"What's more important? That the parents trust me or the kids?"

"I'm sorry, Claire, but this suspension is immediate."

He said his goodbyes to Matt's folks, then stepped off the porch and crossed the lawn to his car.

"Oh, Claire, I'm so sorry," Mama Ross said. "It's not fair."

It wasn't fair. Nothing about this entire situation was fair. It wasn't right that Luke was dead and she was being persecuted instead of the real villains.

"How can they do this to you?" Matt demanded, his anger needing an outlet.

"They're worried about me being around the kids."

"This is unbelievable. They shouldn't be able to do this."

"They shouldn't be able to, but they did."

Indignation ripped through him. He was ready to take on the entire school board, even the entire community on her behalf if needed, but as he paced the porch and looked at her, she was standing calmly.

"How can you remain so calm?"

Most women would have been screaming at the

outrage or crying over all they'd lost. But he was quickly learning that Claire was no ordinary woman.

"I have to hope this is all part of God's bigger plan. I know He has a plan, and I know I'm a part of it."

"Of course it is," his mother assured her. "God always has a plan."

He shook his head and raked a hand over his face. "I don't understand how you can have such faith."

"I've been through worse and I survived. My faith got me through the most terrible time of my life. I have to trust it will get me through this, as well."

He felt his face redden at her mention of the accident. Yes, she'd been through much worse. Her body may have been battered and broken, but it hadn't broken her spirit. And this time she wouldn't have to go through it alone.

"It's been a very long day. I think I'm going to turn in early." She said her good-nights to everyone, then disappeared into the house, leaving Matt alone on the porch with his parents.

His mother touched his shoulder. "She's right about God having a plan. We're all a part of God's bigger plan."

Anger ripped through him. "I'm tired of hearing about God's plan. Claire doesn't deserve this. She doesn't deserve any of this."

"Jesus didn't deserve to die on the cross for our sins, but He did," his father said.

Matt stopped him. "I didn't come home for a sermon, Dad."

"Why did you come home, Matt? You haven't been here in years and now suddenly you're back. Why are you here, son?"

"Because I thought you both would help me, not judge me."

"No, that's not true. You did think we would judge you. That's why you've stayed away for so long. But then the pressure of suffering got too high and you returned to the ones you knew were always there for you. You came home despite your fear of being judged. Can't you see it's the same way with God? Sometimes He allows our suffering in order to bring us back home, back to Him."

"But Claire is the one suffering, and as far as I can see she hasn't strayed from God. She's stood strong in her faith through all of this, yet she continues to suffer."

"Maybe her suffering isn't meant to return her home. Maybe it's meant for you."

"Me?"

"You've suffered alone for all these years, son. It's only now when someone you care for so much is in trouble that you've been drawn back home."

His folks went inside and left him on the porch to ponder what his father had said. Was it true? Was Claire suffering because it was the only way God could draw him back home? Back to Him?

Anger burned through him at that thought, but it had worked, hadn't it? He had been pulled back. He'd prayed for the first time in years. He'd begun reading his Bible again. But it wasn't right. It wasn't right that Claire had to pay for his foolishness.

But if it would stop this descent that was happening to Claire, would he give up his anger and his bitterness and surrender himself to God again?

* * *

Saturday morning, Claire slept later than she'd planned on, but she hadn't realized how worn-out she was. The stresses of this week had definitely taken a toll on her. She showered and dressed, then went to join in with the rest of the family for breakfast.

She was surprised to find Preston standing in the living room with Matt when she went downstairs. They both turned and Preston's face was grim as he approached them. Claire grimaced. Was he here to arrest her again?

But his reason for coming was much worse than she'd imagined.

"Jessica Alvarez's mother was at the precinct early this morning. Jessica went out last night and was supposed to be back by midnight. She still hasn't returned home."

Claire felt as if she'd been punched. Her heart fell and she felt sick. Jessica was missing?

Matt was quickly by her side, which was a good thing because her knees were about to buckle.

"We'll find her," Matt assured her.

Preston continued. "We don't normally take missing-person reports so soon, but Mrs. Alvarez also told me about a conversation she and Jessica had with you two last night about Principal Spencer being a killer?"

"That's right," Matt told him. "Jessica confided in us that she saw Luke and Spencer together. She thought he might be Luke's supplier…and his killer."

Preston's face hardened at the news. "Why didn't you tell me?"

"We wanted to check him out first. I've got my

guys doing a thorough background on him. I was going to phone you today."

Preston raked a hand through his hair. Claire could see he was irritated about not being kept in the loop and she felt bad for not including him.

"I am still the law in this town, Matt. And I know your DEA investigation has been halted. If you're trying to alienate LPD, you're doing a good job."

"I don't want to exclude you, Preston. I have nothing but the highest respect for the officers, but you're all convinced you have the killer and you're wrong. Claire is being set up and I intend to find out who is behind it even if it costs me my job at the DEA."

Preston eyed Claire. "You knew about this and you didn't call me, either."

"It was just last night," Claire told him. "I haven't had a chance to call you."

Preston shook his head as he gave her a mournful expression. "No, you chose to keep it from me." He stomped out of the house, slamming the door as he left.

He was right. She'd made the choice to trust Matt over Preston. She knew she'd hurt Preston and that saddened her. He had been a good friend to her, someone she could always depend on. But she had to admit she'd never trusted him the way she did Matt.

Then it hit her…she trusted Matt.

"Did we do the right thing?" she asked him.

"We did what we had to do," he said. "Besides, we have a bigger problem now than hurt feelings. We have to find out what happened to Jessica."

"Do you think he would harm her?"

Matt looked as if he wanted to reassure her, but

he knew what she knew—if Principal Spencer was the drug supplier, he'd already murdered one student. He probably wouldn't hesitate to kill another to keep her from talking.

Matt and Claire drove around town and checked out all the places Claire knew the kids hung out. They were hoping to spot Jessica at one of these places, still praying that she wasn't missing because someone discovered she'd been talking to them.

They stopped and talked to as many teens as they could, but Claire knew it was a futile attempt. It was still early on a Saturday evening and many of the kids' hangouts wouldn't get crowded until much later.

"Do they still hang out at the lake?" Matt asked.

"I think so. Let's try there next."

He nodded and drove, parking next to the area that housed picnic tables overlooking the water. It was deserted, which struck Claire as odd. It was the beginning of spring and usually this park ground would be busy with kids hanging out and swimming. But the unusual nip in the air must have been keeping them away. April in Tennessee didn't always bring with it warmer temps right away. They'd been known to have a cold spell as late as the end of April.

Matt sighed. "I'm going to call Garrett and Josh and see if they've found anything." He pulled out his phone and looked at it. "My battery's dead. Can I borrow your phone, Claire?"

She took her phone from her purse, then handed it to Matt. She wandered away from him while he made the call, heading along the bank to a place that had been sectioned off with rocks. The water rolled

over it, causing a small but lovely man-made waterfall. She closed her eyes and listened as water hit
water, the sound soothing and calm. She slipped off
her shoes and dipped her toes into the water. It was
cool as it splashed against her feet. She often came
here to this waterfall whenever she needed to clear
her head or think—that is when it wasn't overrun with
schoolkids. It was a relaxing place to wind down and
enjoy the serenity of the outdoors.

Matt approached from behind her, pulling Claire
back to reality.

"I talked to Garrett. They found Wilson, but they
weren't able to convince him to give up his supplier.
All he would say was he worked for a drug runner
out of Nashville." He sat down on the bank beside
her. "Didn't you tell me Spencer came here from
Nashville?"

"He did, but that doesn't make him the drug dealer
Wilson was talking about."

"Well, they also went through his financials line
by line. He's been making large deposits into his bank
account."

"How large?"

"Larger than someone on a high school principal's salary could afford. But he's been smart. He's
kept all the deposits under the $10,000 mark so the
bank didn't flag them as suspicious. Anything over
$10,000, the banks have to report."

She was devastated to hear this new development.
It seemed Spencer was involved after all. Claire didn't
understand how someone who had dedicated his life to
helping students could also be selling drugs to them.

"I know this is a lot for you to take in," Matt said. "He's your friend."

"He's more than that. He's been my moral compass for several years now. I've counted on him—we've all counted on him—to keep the school going. And he's made great strides academically. Lakeshore has one of the top-ranked science programs in the state. And now to think that he's been conspiring against me? That he killed Luke? That he attacked me?" She shook her head. "I still can't believe it."

He put his arm around her and pulled her toward him. "I know it's hard. I'm sorry."

"Preston was right."

"About what?"

"People do hide. I always try to see the world for good, but people aren't always what they seem, are they?"

"No, I guess they're not. But you are, Claire. There's nothing counterfeit about you. You're just as beautiful and kind a person as you appear to be."

She enjoyed hearing him say so, but she knew it wasn't true. She had a daily struggle to hold back her bitterness and anger over the state of her life. She had to fight for every accomplishment and every day against debilitating pain in order to make something of her life. Often, more than often actually, her anger railed against Matt. He'd gone off to have a successful career, while she'd been left behind to suffer alone.

Alone.

That was the real rub. She could have endured the pain and rehab necessary from the wreck, but why had she had to do it alone? She looked at him now and knew she'd never truly forgiven him for that. The wreck wasn't really his fault, but leaving had been.

"Why did you do it?" she asked him.

"Do what?"

"Why did you leave? I mean I know the accident was terrible and I looked horrible and you probably didn't want to spend your life with a cripple, but you didn't even say goodbye. You just left."

He was shaking his head. "I never thought you looked horrible, Claire. You were beautiful then and you're beautiful now. And I never once thought of you as a cripple."

"Then why did you leave me? You left me alone, Matt. You broke my heart and that hurt so much more than my physical injuries ever did."

"I know. I'm sorry. I was young and scared, but I'm here now, Claire. I should have fought harder when you wouldn't see me. I should have waited it out."

"What do you mean that I wouldn't see you? You never came to the hospital, not even once. My father told me so."

"Your father told me you didn't want to see me."

What was he talking about? "I never said that. I cried for weeks because you didn't come."

His expression hardened and he rubbed his face. "I should have known. He kept me from seeing you."

She shook her head, dismayed but not surprised at her father's actions. Yet she also knew they couldn't blame him for his behavior.

"Now that we know the truth, can we put that behind us, Claire? Can you ever forgive me? Can we go back to the way it used to be between us before that terrible night?"

She stared out at the water and thought about what he was asking. A part of her longed to go backward in time and recapture the love they'd once shared, but another part of her couldn't put the past completely at rest. "The first time you told me you loved me we were sitting on that rock over there, remember?" She pointed to a cluster of rocks along the bank of the lake.

"I remember."

"I can't stop going places that bring back memories. If I did, I would never leave my house. Everywhere I go in Lakeshore, I remember you. I remember some distant moment that I told myself I'd forgotten. And since you've come back, a hundred more memories are flooding through my mind every moment of every day."

They'd picnicked on a blanket here under the stars, holding hands and planning their life together.

"I thought you said it didn't bother you. You said you'd walked the halls and the hangouts and you'd moved past it."

She glared at him for throwing her own words back at her. "Well, it does bother me, Matt."

He was behind her before she realized it, caressing her arms and pulling her toward him. "It bothers me, too. There's not a place in this town that doesn't remind me of you, Claire. Of us."

She turned and was in his arms and his lips found hers and her heart soared. In his arms was the only place she wanted to be, the only place she'd ever wanted to be. Yet she pushed away from him, shaking her head. "I can't do it. I can't go through that again."

"Go through what again?"

"I forgive you for leaving me, Matt. I know you're not the same person you were back then. But I'm not that same girl I was, either. I've been through too much. I just can't risk getting hurt that way again."

She hurried away from him, heading back to the car.

It was hard walking away from him, refusing him when he was opening his heart to her. But she felt she was making the right decision.

Their time together had ended long ago.

EIGHT

Despite what was going on with Jessica and with Claire's suspension, Claire was thankful Alisa was gracious enough to invite her to the bridal shower being held at the Ross home Sunday afternoon. Not only was it better than sitting alone in her room while Matt went with the rest of the men involved in the wedding to get fitted for tuxedos, but she was glad to see a true love unfolding. She was happy for Alisa, even though seeing her that way made Claire's heart ache for what might have been between her and Matt.

She helped Mama Ross set up the punch and cake and hang the decorations, then enjoyed the conversation and companionship of the other women who arrived. Claire found it simple and normal to have something nice to think about for a while and it helped, if only briefly, to take her mind off her own problems. She couldn't remember the last time she'd felt as if she belonged more than she did today. Alisa and the Ross family had surely welcomed her in just as they had ten years earlier.

Claire heard someone calling her name and looked up to see Preston standing in the doorway beside Mama Ross.

"Detective Ware would like to speak with you, Claire," she said.

He motioned for her to join him in the kitchen.

"Thank you," Claire told her. She walked into the kitchen. "What are you doing here?" she demanded.

"I'm just checking up on you."

"I'm okay. I'm trying to keep my mind off my troubles today and enjoy spending time with Alisa and her friends and family. For a few hours anyway, I can pretend everything is normal in my life."

A ding on her phone indicated a text message. "That's probably Matt checking up on me, too," she said. "He had to go across town with the rest of the men for tux fitting." She took out her phone and opened her message.

It wasn't from Matt.

This is Jessica. I need your help, Miss Kendall. Can you come get me?

Her initial excitement at hearing from Jessica was tempered with worry. "It's from Jessica. She's in trouble."

Claire texted her back. Where are you? Are you okay?

I'm at the school. Can you come get me?

"We have to help her," Claire said, but Preston was already shaking his head.

"The last time you received a text message like that from a student, you found Luke dead and became the killer's next target. Then I had to arrest you. How can you be sure this isn't another trap?"

"I can't. But I also can't ignore her cry for help, can I?"

Preston raked a hand over his face. "I'll go. You stay here and I'll call you when I find Jessica. Okay?"

She agreed. It seemed a logical solution. However, a half hour later when she still hadn't heard from Preston, she grew worried.

She tried to call Preston, but he didn't respond. Finally, she texted Jessica again asking if Preston had arrived.

Again, she received the same type of frantic text from Jessica.

Please help me, Miss Kendall. I'm scared.

Claire hesitated. Preston was right. The last time she'd gotten a text like this from a student, she'd found Luke dead. Matt had assured her that Luke had been dead too long to have sent that text. Was this another trap? How could she be sure this was Jessica and not someone who'd harmed the girl and taken her phone? And where was Preston and why wasn't he answering his phone?

She quickly hit the call button. She wasn't going there until she heard Jessica's voice. When it went straight to voice mail, she texted back that she wasn't coming until she could speak to Jessica to ensure it was her and not a trap.

She dialed again and this time Jessica's raspy voice answered after the second ring. "Miss Kendall?"

Claire was thankful to hear the girl's voice. "Jessica? Are you all right?"

Her answer was interrupted when a male voice pulled the phone from her. "She's fine…for now."

Claire thought she recognized that voice, but she couldn't be sure. Anger bit through her. "Who is this? If you hurt her—"

"It's not her I want, Claire, and I think you know that. There's a car parked outside. Stay on the phone with me as you walk out and get into it. Don't speak to anyone. Don't alert anyone. If you do, I'll put a bullet in Jessica's head and you can have two students' deaths on your hand."

She definitely recognized his voice now. It was Principal Spencer. "Don't hurt her," Claire told him. "I'll do as you say."

Claire sucked in a breath, then sneaked out the back door. A beige sedan was parked at the curb and Claire spotted Ryan leaning against it.

She approached him, disappointed that her suspicions were true and he had filled Luke's shoes. But had Luke ever kidnapped someone or threatened to kill them? Ryan sheepishly held out his hand for her phone.

"Why are you doing this?" she asked him.

"I have no choice," he told her, then took the phone and let the caller know they were on their way.

Claire knew she should remain quiet as he drove, but she couldn't let Ryan go down this path without trying to reason with him. He was only a boy—a boy who was in way over his head in criminal activity.

"You don't have to do this, Ryan. You can still

get out of this. Let me call my friend Matt. He's a DEA agent."

"He can't help me, Miss Kendall. No one can. They killed Luke. They'll kill me, too."

"Ryan, did you hurt Jessica?"

"No." He seemed insulted that she would even suggest such a thing.

"What about me? Someone has been trying to kill me. Was that you?"

"No. I don't want to hurt anyone."

She understood. He'd started this venture as a fun activity for the popularity and possibly the money, but it had turned darker faster than he'd ever thought it could. Unfortunately for Ryan, it was only going to get worse for him if he continued to be involved with the drug ring.

"You may not want to, but what will you do when they insist? When they threaten to kill you? Who would you harm to save your own life?"

He gripped the steering wheel, but she could see the wheels turning in his head. "I don't know," he admitted, "but it's too late for me." He pulled into the school parking lot and stopped the car by the southwest doors. "They're waiting for us in your old classroom."

He took her arm and led her down the hall. The school was still and quiet as they approached her classroom. The crime scene tape had been pulled off and the overhead light was on. As they reached the door, Claire spotted Jessica perched on top of a desk. "Jessica!" she cried, rushing into the room and hugging the girl.

Jessica clung to her. "I'm so sorry, Miss Kendall. I was so scared."

"I know, but it's going to be okay. We're going to get out of this."

"Don't be too sure about that," a male voice stated behind them. Principal Spencer stepped from the corner, essentially blocking their only escape route. She remembered another time he'd crouched in the corner lying in wait for her. The day he'd murdered Luke. She was sure now it had been Spencer who'd killed him. Ryan might have stepped in for Luke, but Claire could see he hadn't yet graduated to violence.

Spencer held a gun in his hand pointed at them. Ryan handed him Claire's cell phone, then walked out as Spencer quickly pocketed the phone. "So happy you could join us, Claire."

Gone was the pleasant, concerned man she'd thought she knew.

What had happened to Preston? Had Spencer caught him snooping around the school and hurt him—or worse? She hugged Jessica tighter against her, wishing she'd been able to alert Matt to her predicament. He would return from the tux shop not knowing where she'd gone. By the time he realized something was wrong, would it be too late for her and Jessica?

Matt was antsy. He didn't like leaving Claire for this long. He didn't like being out of touch with her. He tried her phone several times, then dialed the house phone. His mother answered, and when he asked to speak to Claire, her voice faltered.

"I'm not sure where she is right now. She was just here. I'll have her call you back."

He tried her cell phone again, and each time it went to voice mail, his worry grew. "I have to go," he told his father.

"What is it? What's wrong?"

"It's Claire. She's not answering. I'll meet you all back at the house."

He took off and jumped into the car, not caring that his family probably thought he was nuts. He had no reason to suspect anything was wrong, but it didn't strike him as right that she wasn't responding to his calls or texts. Something had happened. He felt it in his gut.

It was at least forty-five minutes back to the house from the tux shop and he continued dialing Claire's phone and continued to get the voice mail.

Each minute that he didn't hear anything felt like an hour. He buzzed through town, laying on his horn and whizzing around cars on the interstate. He had to reach her. If something had happened to her...

He shook that thought away. He couldn't dwell on it. He couldn't go there. What he wouldn't give right now to have her call him and tell him he was overreacting or that her phone hadn't held a charge.

His phone rang and Matt's heart jumped into his throat until he saw it was Preston calling, not Claire.

"We have a problem," Preston told him. "Claire received a text message from Jessica asking her to come get her."

Matt's heart clenched. It had to be a trap. "And she went." It wasn't a question. He already knew. If

Jessica was in trouble, Claire wasn't the type to sit around and wait for help to arrive.

"I told her to let me handle it, but I guess she didn't listen. I went to the school and couldn't find her. By the time I got back to your folks' house, Claire was gone. I traced her cell phone to an abandoned factory on the outskirts of town. She must have gotten another text from Jessica and gone after her."

"I'm ten minutes out," Matt said when Preston told him the location.

"I'm already on my way," Preston added. "I'll meet you there."

Matt hung up and said a prayer that God would keep Claire safe until he could get to her.

"I'm sorry," Jessica told her as they huddled together while Principal Spencer paced from one side of the room to the other, the gun ever present in his hand. "He's the one who sent that text to you." She choked over the words. "He really is the one who killed Luke."

Claire had already figured all that out. She'd walked into Principal Spencer's trap twice now and she didn't like being played for a fool. It sickened her to know that a professional educator, someone who was supposed to be looking out for the well-being of his students, was not only involved with selling drugs to those students, but had also killed one and kidnapped another and framed Claire for murder. Principal Spencer's list of atrocities was growing every moment. Would he hesitate to kill her and Jessica, too? She doubted it.

He seemed anxious as he paced back and forth

in the room, the gun remaining gripped in his hand. Was he realizing the trouble he was in? Maybe she could talk some sense into him.

"You won't get away with this," Claire warned him. "Matt will come for me and so will Preston. If you do anything to hurt us, you'll have to answer to them."

He shook his head as if he didn't care and only continued the pacing.

Maybe she should try reasoning with him. He had once aspired to help kids, not to injure them. Perhaps some part of him still did. "Bill, I know you don't want to hurt Jessica. Things have just gotten out of hand. I'm sure if you put the gun down and release us, we can figure a way out of this."

He ignored her, checking his watch again. Was he waiting for something to happen? For someone?

Claire hugged Jessica to her protectively. "We're going to be fine," she told the girl. She wished Matt were here. She wished she'd called or texted him before she'd come. Would he somehow figure out where she was and what had happened?

Mostly, she watched Principal Spencer pace and tried to remain calm by remembering that they weren't alone. God was watching out for them and He would surely send help.

Matt keyed the address Preston gave him into his GPS and followed the instructions. He spotted Preston's unmarked car parked to the side of what looked like an abandoned building in a seedier part of town. He pulled up beside it and cut the engine, getting out to meet him.

"This is where Claire came to meet Jessica? What is this place?"

"The old garment factory. It's been abandoned since they went out of business years ago. Jessica's probably been squatting here since she vanished, hiding out."

Matt shared Preston's trepidation after seeing this building. Why would Claire have come to this place alone? She should have waited for one of them to go with her. He prayed she was safe, but pulled his weapon in case she wasn't.

"Where's Claire's car?"

"I don't know, but her cell phone is pinging from inside. She's definitely in there." He pulled out his weapon and kept it in his hand, prepared for anything.

Matt did the same, but he felt he owed Preston something for all they'd been through. "Thanks for looking out for Claire."

Preston met his eye. "I told you when we met that I would do anything for Claire. I meant it."

Matt couldn't help being glad Claire had a friend like Preston.

They stopped at the front of the building and Preston stepped aside so Matt could enter first. He raised his weapon and scanned the long building. He heard Preston behind him.

"It's empty," he said.

They moved the length of the building, then Preston pointed to a door. Matt opened it and they rushed inside.

The main room had tables lined up along with makeshift drug paraphernalia, but no one was inside.

Matt gazed at the instruments. "Looks like a drug house that's been abandoned recently.

Preston motioned toward another door. "I'll cover you."

Matt returned his gun to its holster and used both hands to pull open the large metal doors as Preston trained his gun on the opening, ready for anything. The enclosed room was dark but Matt shined a light down into the basement. It, too, was empty. This place was a dead end. Whoever had been here was long gone, but did that include Claire and Jessica? Had she convinced the girl to leave with her? That explained why her car wasn't here, but not why her phone was pinging here or why she wasn't answering his calls.

"Nothing," he said.

"I wouldn't say that," Preston told him.

Matt turned as Preston barreled down on him with what looked like a shovel. It smacked Matt's head and blinding pain ripped through him. He dropped his flashlight and fought to stand, but his knees buckled under the pain.

He lifted his face again and saw Preston readying for another swing. Matt reached up a hand but couldn't deflect the second blow. It rammed into the side of his head and sent him reeling.

As the room began to dim around him, Preston knelt beside him and flashed Matt a sardonic smile. "I told you, Matt. I would do anything for Claire. Anything."

NINE

Claire eyed the storage cabinet. Unlike the lab, this room didn't hold any chemicals she could use to free them, but if she could get closer, perhaps she could find something that might help them out of this as she'd done before. But this storage cabinet was locked tight.

Spencer caught her gaze and grinned. "You didn't think I would fall for that twice, did you?"

Claire eyed him. "So it was you who attacked me in the lab?"

"Yes, it was me. I didn't get a chance to tell you how impressed I was at your ingenuity. That stuff burned like crazy."

She was glad it had burned, and wished it had done more damage. Her hand immediately went to her throat. If she hadn't been able to escape, she would be just as dead as Luke now.

She looked at Jessica and knew they were in very real danger from this man.

He fidgeted anxiously in front of the windows. Every now and then he pulled down a slat of the blind and peered out. What was he doing? If he was trying to frighten them, it was working. Jessica quivered in her arms and sobbed quietly. She looked as if she'd lost all hope of making it out of this alive. But Claire had not given up. She used the opportunities when Spencer was distracted at the window to scan the room for something, anything, to defend themselves.

She jumped at the sound of his phone buzzing. Principal Spencer pulled it out and glanced at the screen. He paled, then put away the phone and picked up the gun.

The tension in the room changed. Spencer's demeanor morphed from nervous and waiting to resigned. Claire's heart kicked up with fear and Jessica whimpered and pressed herself closer to Claire. Something was happening. It was apparent that call had been the one Principal Spencer had been waiting for.

He gulped with anxiety, and it was clear this wasn't the route he'd wanted to take. "I didn't want this," he stated to them. "I didn't want Luke to die, but you—" he pointed the gun at Claire "—you convinced him to stop peddling for us. He said he wanted out, but no one gets out. I didn't want to kill him, but it wasn't my decision."

Now Claire understood. Principal Spencer wasn't the man in charge. He wasn't the drug supplier they'd been searching for. He was just a middleman caught up in the web. He had killed Luke—he'd just admitted he'd done it—but it had been on someone else's orders.

"I'm sorry, Claire, but you got too close to the operation and it's not up to me anymore. I do as I'm told."

Jessica wailed and sobbed with fear, but Claire clutched her as Spencer raised the gun and readied it to fire. His hand shook and that worried Claire even more. Should she rush him? Should she try to give Jessica an opportunity to escape? She steeled herself for the confrontation. This man disgusted her. He wasn't even the man in charge. He was a nothing, a lackey who did the dirty work for someone else.

"Get ready to run," she whispered to Jessica, then pulled away from the girl and stood to face him, steeling herself against her own fear. "You disgust me," she told Spencer. "Preying on children, students whom you were supposed to protect. You make me sick."

His hand shook even more as he aimed the gun at her. "I'm sorry, Claire."

"You're sorry? You're sorry for killing Luke? You're sorry for terrorizing Jessica and holding us hostage and threatening our lives? You'll never be sorry enough." She rushed at him, grabbing for the gun and simultaneously yelling, "Run!" to Jessica.

She struggled with him for control of the gun but he spotted Jessica heading for the door and panicked, his finger pulling down on the trigger. The gun fired and that seemed to bring them both to attention. The pitifully timid man vanished and he must have realized he had no choice now but to barrel through. He straightened and shoved Claire, sending her flying. She hit the wall with a thud and waves of pain rolled over her. He yelled for Jessica to stop and fired again when she didn't. Claire heard her scream and saw her rush out the door as a bullet whizzed past her head and lodged into the wall behind her.

Claire screamed and jumped on him to keep him from going after Jessica. She would fight him until Jessica was safe. She clawed at his face and he struggled to pull her off and regain his solid footing.

He finally managed to throw her off, sending her flying again. This time she hit the floor, which knocked the breath out of her. He turned to her, raised the gun and aimed it to shoot. But before he could, she heard a male voice call out.

"Lower your weapon now!"

Her heart hammered at the thought that Matt had come to rescue her, but Claire saw it was Preston there with his own gun raised and pointed at Spencer.

Spencer started to turn and Preston fired several shots that sent the man toppling toward her. Claire scrambled out of the way as he hit the floor very near to her, his frozen face registering shock at his last, final moment.

Preston moved through the classroom and stood over him, kicking the gun from the still man's hand, then bent and felt for a pulse. Claire was certain he wouldn't find one. She saw the life spill out of Bill Spencer as he lay only a foot away from her.

Preston turned to her, then scooped her up in his arms, hugging her tightly. "Did he hurt you?"

"No, I'm fine. Jessica!" She realized she didn't know where the girl had run to. Did she know she was now safe? That she didn't have to live in fear of her principal anymore?

"She's fine. I saw her as I was entering the school. I sent her outside to wait for us."

Claire sighed with relief. It was over. It was really over. She was safe. Jessica was safe. Her students were safe. Then she remembered the text message Spencer had received. She was certain he'd been waiting on someone. And he'd said he didn't want to kill her but hadn't had a choice. It wasn't over. There was someone even worse out there.

She told Preston, and he searched the body and pulled out a cell phone. He checked the text messages. "I'll run the number, although it will no doubt be a burner phone." He pocketed the phone, then helped Claire to her feet. "Let's get out of here. I need to call this in and have the room secured. There'll be an investigation, since I fired my weapon and killed a man."

She was suddenly concerned about Preston. "I'll tell them and so will Jessica. You saved us. Preston, you saved us both."

A big grin spread across his face at her words. "Then it was all worth it."

He put his arm around her and walked out. Claire was thankful to see Jessica safe, but she also couldn't help but wonder, where was Matt? She couldn't wait to relate to him all that had happened today and how they were one step closer to finding the drug dealer they'd been searching for.

A heavy weight seemed to be holding him down as Matt regained consciousness. He tried to lift his head but it took all his strength to do so. His eyes fluttered open and, once they cleared, he took in the room. He was underground, some kind of basement no doubt. And his hands and legs were bound.

Memories rushed back to him. Preston had cold-cocked him and tied him up down here. But where was Claire? They'd been on their way to find her. Preston had said she'd walked right into a trap. Anger bit through Matt as he realized he'd been the one to walk into a trap… Preston's trap. There was no emergency. Claire hadn't been in danger. Although he couldn't be sure she wasn't now.

He'd been ambushed…again. This betrayal took him back to the ambush against his ranger team. He'd lost men then, good men with families. Who would he lose now because of this attack? Claire? He wouldn't allow it.

He struggled with the binds, frustrated when he couldn't loosen them. He was trapped and Claire was depending on him.

He took a deep breath. He could do nothing to help himself, but he had to remember he wasn't alone. He was never alone. It was something Claire had helped to remind him of. He tried to control his fear and to trust in the Lord.

"Lord, Claire is in trouble. I need Your help. Please keep her safe and help me get out of this."

He used the wall to push himself into a sitting position, then to his knees. Preston had tied his hands behind him with zip ties, but Matt had been trained to escape them. He whipped his hands against his back twice before the zip tie busted apart.

He rubbed his wrists, then surveyed his area. His gun was gone and so was his cell phone. He had no idea how long he'd been unconscious, but his head seemed to have a jackhammer inside it.

He pulled at the door but it wouldn't open and he searched among the other walls. It looked as if that one door was the only way out. He had to get it opened. He listened but didn't hear any movement outside. He used his shoulder to try to push it open. It didn't budge, but that didn't stop him from ramming it again. If opening this door was his only way out, he wouldn't stop until he got it opened.

But where was Claire? Preston had told him she'd received a text message from Jessica luring her into a trap. Had Preston set that trap, or had it been just a lure to get Matt out of the way? Either way, Claire's life was in danger. The longer she was with Preston without knowing who he was and what he was involved in, the more danger she was in.

Questions rushed through his mind. Was Preston also behind the Trixie ring operating in Lakeshore? Had he killed Luke and tried to kill Claire? He had to warn her about Preston. He'd promised to protect her, but just like his time with the rangers, the enemy had hidden right before his eyes.

He couldn't let her down again.

"Thank you for coming for me, Miss Kendall," Jessica said, giving Claire a hug before running to her mother, who was waiting with open arms.

Claire was happy to see Jessica reunited with her family and safe. She glanced over at Preston, who gazed at her over the roof of his car. Jessica owed her life to Preston, and so did Claire. She was thankful he'd found them in time.

"Ready to go home?" Preston asked her.

She nodded and got back into his car.

"I thought you might want this back," he said, handing her the cell phone Spencer had taken from her.

"Thank you."

"I didn't want you to lose all your contacts."

She checked her phone, hoping to see some message or voice mail from Matt, but there were none. She'd received multiple calls and texts from Preston's phone number, but other than that the last call on her list was the one from Jessica's phone, the call that had started it all. It was odd, though, that Matt hadn't phoned her. He would surely have returned from the tux shop with his family by now and wondered where she'd gone. Wouldn't he wonder if she was in trouble? Wouldn't he at least want to check to make sure she was safe?

He'd been practically pinned to her side for the past week. And today, when she'd actually needed him, he hadn't even phoned her?

Weird.

She glanced up and saw Preston was heading out of town toward his house. "Why are we going to your house instead of the Rosses'?"

"If you're right and Spencer was just the middleman, you'll be safer at my house."

"Preston, I appreciate—"

"He could have killed you, Claire. This time, I'm not taking no for an answer."

She didn't bother protesting any further. "I should let Matt know my plans," she said, opening her phone.

"He knows."

"You spoke to him?"

"Sure. He's checking out a lead out of town. He'll be gone for a while. He asked me to watch after you."

That struck her as odd. Why hadn't he called or texted her to let her know he was leaving town? "Does he know what happened with Principal Spencer?"

"Absolutely, we discussed it. When we realized Spencer was only a middleman, he said following up on this lead for Spencer's boss was his top priority."

Claire felt as if she'd been slapped by his indifference. Had he really said that? But why would Preston lie about Matt's actions, and why hadn't Matt told her so himself?

"He's DEA, Claire. You knew he was only in town to ferret out the Trixie ring."

She sank into her seat. She had known that was why Matt had come to town, but her naive, hapless self had hoped something else, that true love would make him stay. Warmth spread through her face. Had she been a first-class fool for Matt Ross? Again?

When they arrived at Preston's, he led her to a guest bedroom. "You'll be safe here," he promised. "At least until we can figure out who is behind this all."

She barely saw the room. Her only thoughts were of Matt and what a fool she'd been. Had he stayed after the DEA closed the investigation because he was worried about her or, as Preston insinuated, because he wanted to bust this drug ring?

Preston must have noticed her sadness because he placed his hands on her shoulders and looked down into her face. "I know he's hurt you, but I will never leave you, Claire. I will always be here for you." He planted a kiss on her forehead, then walked out and left her alone to rest.

She tried Matt's phone again and it went straight to voice mail. She left another message asking where he was, then texted him again. She was growing more and more worried with each unanswered call. Where was he? And was he safe? And that annoying, planted doubt crept back in… Was he ignoring her calls and texts because he really didn't want her?

She glanced at her phone and saw a number she didn't recognize in her phone list. She remembered Matt had used her phone to call his ranger friend Garrett. Was he in contact with Matt? Would he even answer her call? She didn't know, but she had to try.

She pushed on the number and her phone dialed. Soon a click sounded and a male voice answered. "Hello."

"Hi, Garrett, it's Claire."

"Hey, Claire."

"I was wondering if you'd talked to Matt recently. I haven't been able to contact him and I'm really concerned about him."

"How long has he been out of touch?"

"He went to go check out a lead on our drug dealer, but he's not answering his phone or responding to text messages. I was wondering if you'd spoken to him this afternoon."

"I haven't, but I'll try to contact him. Stay by the phone. I'll call you right back."

She hung up, confident that Garrett would somehow be able to do what she could not. She turned and saw Preston standing behind her, leaning against the door frame. She hadn't even heard the bedroom door open. How long had he been standing there watching and listening? And why had he sneaked up on her?

"You startled me," she told him.

"Who were you talking to?"

"An army friend of Matt's. I've tried calling him several times, but each time it goes straight to voice mail. I'm getting worried about him, so I wanted to see if his friend had heard from him."

"I told you not to worry about Matt. He can take care of himself."

"I know, but why isn't he answering my call?"

Preston sighed, the irritation in his voice obvious. "I didn't want to tell you this, Claire. I wanted to spare you for a while longer."

"Spare me from what?"

"Matt isn't checking out a lead. He's gone. He left town."

"What do you mean?"

"I mean, he's gone back to where he came from. He left you, Claire. He left you just when you needed him."

She shook her head. She didn't believe it. "He wouldn't do that."

"He already did it. Twice! Why is it so hard to believe? He's done it before, left you when you needed him."

She sucked in a breath, stunned by his words and what they meant. Matt wouldn't leave her, would he? He'd promised her he wouldn't. But why had he told Preston he was leaving? And why wasn't he responding to her call?

Hot tears pressed against her. This could not be happening again. She'd let her guard down. She'd let Matt in again despite promising herself she wouldn't.

Preston's face softened and he approached her, his arms outstretched. He pulled her into a hug. "I didn't want to tell you. I know how much he's hurt you, but I'm here, Claire. I've always been here for you. I will never leave you and I promise I will always protect you."

She let Preston hug her, but she couldn't let herself be comforted by his words. She didn't want to believe Matt was gone, and she didn't.

Nothing except hearing it from his own lips would convince Claire that Matt had left her.

She phoned Garrett back and repeated what Preston had told her.

Garrett was adamant that it wasn't true. "Matt would never leave you. He's crazy about you."

She believed he wouldn't leave, but it felt good to hear Garrett confirm it. They were no longer frightened teenagers. Matt had grown into a man who didn't walk away from danger, especially when it included someone he cared for.

"But why would Preston tell me that?"

"I don't know, but no one else has heard from Matt, either. I don't like that. I think he's in trouble. I'm going to see if I can track his cell phone. If it's turned on, I should be able to get a location. I'll be in touch."

Claire's mind whirled as she hung up with Garrett. She prayed Matt was safe. But why would Preston tell her that Matt had left her? She knew he wasn't fond of Matt, but if he was truly in trouble surely Preston didn't dislike him so much that he would allow something bad to happen to Matt without intervening. Her mind couldn't process that Preston would be so cold...although he had been very threatened by Matt.

This was crazy. She was talking about the man who'd just saved her and Jessica's lives. He'd arrived at the school just in time to keep Principal Spencer from shooting them both, and he'd been forced to kill the man to prevent that. After all Preston had done, she shouldn't be doubting his intentions.

Yet she did.

She couldn't deny the facts. She didn't believe Matt had left her, but Preston claimed he had. One of them was wrong, and she wasn't ready to give up on Matt.

She dialed Matt's number again, hoping and praying this time for a response. She heard Preston in the other room and headed toward him. She had to convince him that he was wrong about Matt and persuade him to help her find him.

She pushed open the sliding door and saw him pull a phone from his pocket. He took it out and looked at it, then shook his head, a flash of anger on his face before he pushed the button to send it to voice mail, then slid it back into his pocket. The ringing on her phone stopped and it went to voice mail and she heard Matt's soft baritone telling her to leave a message.

She stepped back through the doorway and let the phone disconnect as she processed what she'd just seen. It had to be coincidence, didn't it, that the phone in Preston's pocket rang at the same time she'd called Matt's and that her call went to voice mail right as he pushed the button? She couldn't see the phone in his hand clearly, but it had been an iPhone and she was certain Matt had an iPhone. But then so did Preston. So did she. She told herself she was being ridiculous, but she couldn't help redialing Matt's number just to make certain.

She peeked around the door frame again and spotted Preston. As the phone began to ring in her ear, she heard a buzzing sound coming from his pocket. He pulled out the phone again and she heard him mutter her name under his breath before pressing the button again to send it to voice mail. In her ear, the line went right to Matt's familiar voice telling her to leave a message.

She moved quickly but quietly away from the door and rushed outside to the back patio, her mind swirling with information she couldn't even begin to process. Was it really true? Had she seen what she thought she'd seen? Did Preston really have Matt's phone? But why would he?

Her phone rang, startling her. She spotted Garrett's number pop up and she quickly answered.

"Claire, I pinged Matt's cell phone. I have a location. He's at 270 Northridge Road in Lakeshore."

She sighed, Garrett's words confirming what she already knew. "This is 270 Northridge Road."

"Where are you?"

"I'm at my friend Preston's house. I think I just saw him with Matt's phone. Why would he have Matt's phone? And, more important, why wouldn't he tell me?"

"How well do you trust your friend?"

She wanted to say she trusted him completely, and once upon a time she had. But those words refused to come. "I want to trust him, but I don't know." It was too horrible what she was thinking. She'd known Preston for years. He was a respected member of the Lakeshore police, but logic told her that being a cop was the best cover for a drug dealer. Was it possible Preston was the man behind Spencer, the man who'd ordered Luke killed? Then why burst in and kill his own man to save her life?

She sighed as she realized the truth. Preston was always trying to play the hero.

"I think you should get out of there, Claire."

She wanted to, but she couldn't, not yet. "Not until I know what's happened to Matt."

"How are you going to find that out?"

"I'll search the house. I'm not leaving until I know Matt isn't tied up here somewhere. He could have him stashed in the basement or the garage."

"It would be pretty risky to keep him tied up in the same house with you."

She sighed at the truth. "Preston is nothing if not cocky. He would think since he's a police officer, no one would question him."

"I don't like this," Garrett stated. "Matt will kill me if something happens to you. I'm coming to get you out of there."

"No! Matt knows I make my own decisions."

She disconnected the line and stared back at the house. She wanted nothing more than to flee across the lawn and get away from the man who'd tricked her. She'd gushed and praised him for coming to their rescue, but had Preston's savior act just been a ruse to make himself the hero? She thought so. But how could someone who claimed to care for her also try to kill her and frame her for murder?

She didn't want to go back into that house and pretend everything was fine and that she didn't know that Preston had betrayed her. But she would. If he had Matt stashed somewhere inside, she wouldn't leave this house until she found him.

* * *

Matt leaned against the wall to catch his breath. He'd been pounding away at the door for what seemed like hours and he wasn't making any headway. The door was solid and so far he hadn't been able to budge it.

He raked a hand through his hair, wiping away dirt and sweat. He hadn't felt this alone and vulnerable and out of control since…

…the night of the ambush.

A grenade explosion had sent him flying backward down the mountain, falling several feet, then landing hard on his back, causing the cracked vertebrae he'd sustained along with a fractured ankle. He'd known he should move to find safety, but the pain was just too great. Above him, he'd heard gunfire, rapid at first, then steadily declining in frequency, and he'd wondered if they'd killed everyone already. And if they would soon be coming for him, too.

Still, he hadn't been able to move. He'd just lain in the dirt and stared up at the night sky, the stars shining so brightly against the black canvas. He hadn't known it then, but he was now sure it had been God who'd held him and kept him safe that night.

He thought about that night now as he sat in the dark. The image of the stars shining so brightly had never left him. Now he thought about Joseph and his time in the pit where his brothers had tossed him. Had he looked up, able to see only the stars of the night sky and known God was with him? Thousands of years had passed between them, but Matt knew they'd both been staring at the same sky, the same stars, crying out to the same God in desperation.

He couldn't see the sky where he was now, but he saw it in his mind's eye and was reminded that God had not abandoned him then and He hadn't abandoned him now. As He had with Joseph, God had a plan for Matt's life. He would bring him out of this literal pit and restore him to his family.

He wanted to see Alisa get married. He wanted to see her in her wedding gown and be there when she spoke her vows. He wanted to spend one more day with his parents and tell them how much he loved them and appreciated all they'd done for him.

But most of all, he wanted one more day with Claire. One more moment where he could see the sparkle in her big blue eyes and feel his heart kick up a notch when she smiled up at him. He longed for one more chance to take her into his arms and let her know his love for her had never faltered, even if he had. For the first time in a long while, he looked forward to his future because of her.

Oh, God, I need to tell her I love her, he prayed silently. *I need to show her how beautiful and desirable she is and ask her to be my wife.*

But first he had to get out of his pit.

And he couldn't do it alone. He'd given it everything he'd had and failed. He had no control over his own future and that frightened him, but it also was a painful relief. He set down the burden of escape like a weight he'd been carrying on his shoulders. Nothing he did could rescue him from this basement.

Instead, he gave the matter to God and waited.

TEN

Claire feigned a headache and told Preston she needed to go lie down in the spare bedroom. He offered to bring her some pain reliever, but she waved him away, insisting all she needed was sleep.

Once in the guest room, she grabbed extra pillows from the closet and stuffed them beneath the blankets, trying to make it look like a person sleeping. It wouldn't fool Preston if he stepped into the room, but maybe it would fool him long enough for her to search the house to make sure he didn't have Matt tied up somewhere.

She opened the door cautiously and peered out. The hallway was clear and she could hear Preston's voice from the study below. She started on the top floor, searching the bedrooms and not expecting to find anything, but she had to check them regardless. She heard Preston in the study speaking on the phone, so she snuck down the back stairs to check out the basement.

She pushed open the heavy door but found nothing out of the ordinary, no signs of Matt or any indication he'd been there. But then did she even know what it was she was looking for except to stumble across Matt himself?

She went back upstairs and decided to check the garage next. She tiptoed through the kitchen to the garage entrance. She saw nothing, so she searched through the storage room, still finding nothing. She opened the door to Preston's car and scanned inside, looking for some clue, any clue that might lead her to Matt's whereabouts.

She went back inside, worried that she was finding nothing. Was she wrong about Preston? Was she jumping to conclusions? After all, Preston was the one person who had always been there for her.

She leaned against the kitchen counter, contemplating what to do. She lifted her head and saw the wooden knife block, identical to the one in Claire's kitchen, tucked into a corner. Only, this one had all the knives present.

Identical to the one in her kitchen.

That sinking feeling hit Claire again, but she couldn't resist reaching for the chef's knife, grabbing its cold, metal handle and pulling it out. Her heart sank when she saw the slightly bent tip of the knife where she'd used it to pry open a can of peaches and had never been able to press it back straight. It suddenly all made sense to her. Preston had had access to her house. He'd supplied Spencer with his own knife to kill Luke, then replaced it with hers when he'd decided to frame her for the murder. And he would have had an easy time transferring her fingerprints to the murder weapon.

She shuddered, realizing how much planning and preparation her supposed friend had put into framing her for the murder of a student. But had his plan been to eventually find evidence to exonerate her—even if he had to manufacture it—or to let her go to prison for murder?

She thought back to all the times she'd spent with him alone. He'd been the one to tell her that people hid their true selves. She knew now he'd been talking about himself. How long had he been involved in illegal activities? Since she'd known him? Had he come to Lakeshore already a criminal mastermind?

She'd searched the house and it seemed Matt was not being held here. She should phone Garrett to let him know, but she also knew Garrett would insist on her leaving and she couldn't; she wouldn't leave until she knew what Preston had done with Matt. And she was now absolutely convinced that Preston was behind Matt's sudden disappearance.

It was time to confront him outright with her suspicions and demand to know what he'd done with Matt.

She walked into the study, where he was working at his desk.

"Feeling better?" he asked as she sat on the couch and picked up a book, pretending she was going to read it.

"Better," she assured him, wondering if he could see the contempt she now held for him in her eyes.

But how could she get Preston to admit what he'd done? She had an idea. She pulled her phone from her pocket and again dialed Matt's number. It began to ring and so did the phone in Preston's pocket.

He met her eyes as the phone in his pocket continued to ring. Finally, he reached in and pulled it out, pressing the off button.

She moved her phone from her ear and stood to face him. "Why do you have Matt's cell phone?"

He sighed, then scrolled through the call list. "Eight calls, Claire. You've called this phone eight times in the past four hours."

"Why do you have Matt's phone? What did you do to him?"

He stood, too, and approached her. "What did I do to him? How about what he did to me? He swoops back into town after abandoning you and all you can think about is him. He left you, Claire. I've been here for you every day, Claire. I've been here. He hasn't. But even now you can't think of anything but him." He raked a hand over his face, obviously frustrated with her.

But he was right about one thing—all she cared about right now was Matt. "Where is he, Preston? Did you do something to him? Did you hurt him?" She couldn't help the way her voice shrieked at the thought.

He turned to glare at her, rage brimming in his eyes and his breath raspy. He smacked her across the face with the back of his hand, knocking her to the floor. As he stood over her, Claire knew he was capable of real violence and her heart sank. It was true. He had done something to Matt.

She crawled to her feet and faced him again, her cheek stinging and probably red where he'd hit her. "Where is Matt?"

He hit her once more and this time she landed on the couch. His cool composure unraveled. His hands went in the air and he began pacing and muttering. "What else can I do, Claire? I've given you everything you've ever asked me to. I've been here day after day after day and watched you pine after someone who didn't even have the courtesy to call to check on you in ten years. Tell me what else I can do?"

She touched her lip with her finger and it brought back blood. She glared at him again. "You had Luke killed. You gave Spencer the knife and made him kill Luke."

"There are some things you don't mess with, Claire. A man's business is one of them. Luke was a liability. You made Luke a liability. You killed him."

Claire stared up at Preston, seeing him anew for the first time. How could the man she'd known for so long become the monster before her? And, more important, what had he done with Matt?

A noise above him jerked Matt awake. He was still surrounded by darkness, still locked in the basement, but someone was coming.

He leaped to his feet and wiped his hands on his pants to get rid of the sweat and grime. He needed to be sure-handed because whoever walked through that door was going to have to face him. No matter what he had to do, that door would not shut him up inside this basement again.

He pushed himself against the wall, hidden as much from view as he could get when the door opened and someone started down the steps. The light from above cut through the darkness, but all Matt saw was a figure heading down the steps.

The moment the person touched the floor with his foot, Matt grabbed him from behind and locked his arms around his head.

The intruder dropped something—a gun probably—and grabbed Matt's arms, struggling to loosen his grip, but Matt's hold was firm and tight. He shifted his weight and tossed him to the floor.

"No, stop!" His captor's hands were in the air, and his pleading caused Matt to focus on his attacker. It was the boy, Ryan, fearfully staring up at him, his eyes begging for mercy.

Matt's blood boiled at the thought that they'd sent a seventeen-year-old kid to kill him. Preston Ware had reached a new low in Matt's book.

"I didn't come here to hurt you," Ryan said. "I came to let you out."

Matt grabbed for whatever the boy had dropped and saw it was a pair of bolt cutters.

"I cut the lock. I came to release you."

Matt glared at him. He already knew Ryan had replaced Luke as Spencer's lackey. That meant do as you're told or else. "Why?" Matt demanded. He needed to know if this kid was telling the truth.

"Because of Miss Kendall."

Matt's eyes widened, fear suddenly punching him in the gut. "Has something happened to Claire?"

"Detective Ware had her lured to the school, then busted in to play the hero. He shot Principal Spencer, who was supposed to be his partner. When I realized what had happened, I got out of there fast. If he would kill Spencer, I wondered what he would do to me."

"What does this have to do with Claire?"

"She asked me where my line was. What would be so bad that I wouldn't want to do it? Then she told me they would make me do it. I realized she was right. I lost my best friend. I watched someone get shot and

I made a girl I care about cry out of fear for what I might do to her." Matt saw tears form in the kid's eyes. "I don't want to be that person. But Detective Ware is still out there. He's still dangerous. And then I remembered Miss Kendall said you could help. I knew he had locked you down here. Can you do it? Can you stop Detective Ware?"

Matt reached for the boy's hand and pulled him to his feet. This was the mission God had been preparing him for—to stop a drug-dealing killer from preying on anyone else…especially Claire.

"Let's go, kid." Matt ran up the steps and out of the building. He saw a car that he knew had to belong to Ryan. "I'm driving," he said, and Ryan tossed him the keys. As he started the engine, he thought about Garrett and Josh. He would need their help in bringing down Preston, but first he had to warn Claire about the man. "Let me use your cell phone." Ryan handed it over and Matt dialed Claire's phone as they sped away back toward town. It went straight to voice mail.

He then dialed Garrett's number.

"Lewis," came Garrett's strong voice.

"Garrett, it's Matt."

"Where have you been, man?"

"Preston Ware ambushed me. He locked me up in the basement of what looks like an abandoned drug house." Matt shook his head as he scanned the landscape and saw nothing but derelict buildings. He could have screamed for help until his tongue fell out and no one would have heard him. If God hadn't worked on Ryan and given him a change of heart, Matt would surely have died from heat stroke in that basement before someone found him.

Thank You, Lord, for Your mercies.

"I'm heading over there now to confront him. I think Preston is the one behind the Trixie ring and Luke's murder. I have to warn Claire that she can't trust him."

He heard a pause in Garrett's response. "That won't be a problem. She's already fully aware of what he is involved in."

His heart wrenched. "Did he hurt her?"

"No, but he tried to convince her that you'd left her."

Matt's heart caught in his throat at the idea that Claire might believe he'd walked out on her again. She had believed it once before. "How do you know that?"

"She called my number when she couldn't get you to answer."

"Did you tell her it wasn't true? That I wouldn't leave her?"

"I didn't have to tell her, Matt. She knew. She didn't believe him. It seems as if that little ploy was the thing that convinced her he wasn't telling the truth. She was convinced Preston had done something to you, so she started searching the house for clues where he might be hiding you."

His emotions were all over the place. Proud that Claire hadn't believed Preston's lies and that she truly believed in him. But his relief was also flooded with anxiety that she was searching his house.

"You should have pulled her out of there," Matt told Garrett.

"She insisted on staying. She said she wasn't leaving until she knew what had happened to you."

"If he realizes she knows he's lying, there's no telling what he might do."

"Josh and I are staked out in front of the house. So far nothing is—"

He dropped off and Matt overheard Josh commenting on something. "What is it?" Matt asked, wishing this car would go faster. "What's happening?"

"They just walked outside and Preston is carrying a suitcase. He put it in the trunk of his car. Claire looks frightened. He's pushing her into the car. I think he's onto her. He's making his getaway."

Matt pushed the accelerator to the floor and willed the car to go faster, but he knew in his heart he might not make it in time. Once again, he had to give up control.

"Lord, please don't let him hurt her."

Claire huddled against the door, sliding as far away from Preston as she could without climbing out through the window. He must have thought she would try that because he grabbed her arm and yanked her back across the seat.

"Don't try it, Claire," he growled. He pulled the seat belt even tighter around her. His gun was on his lap, close and easily in reach should he need it.

"Where are you taking me?"

"Away."

She shuddered at the sting of his betrayal. "You killed Luke."

"Claire, don't be ridiculous. I haven't killed anyone. Bill Spencer is the killer, not me."

"You made him do it and then you killed him, too."

"I protected you from him. He was going to kill you. I did my job."

"And is it your job to sell drugs to kids? It was my job to protect them from you."

"Stop it, Claire! I said stop it!"

"What did you do to Matt?"

Preston's nostrils flared. "I am sick of hearing about Matt Ross! He's all you care about anymore."

"Where is he, Preston?"

"You want to know if I killed him? Don't worry, Claire. Your precious Matt Ross is alive. I wanted to kill him, but I thought it would be more fun to frame him for Luke's murder instead."

She shook her head. "No one will believe that."

"Everyone will believe it. Trust me, I have it all planned out. I won't have to kill him to ruin his life."

"You wanted to frame him just like you did me."

"I never wanted to frame you, Claire. I thought you would turn to me to protect you. I thought it would bring us closer together. But you didn't. You turned to Matt instead." He spat out Matt's name, his contempt clear.

How had she never noticed the darkness inside Preston? She couldn't, she wouldn't let him get away with this. If he managed to get her out of town, both her and Matt's lives would be ruined.

She reached over and grabbed the wheel. Preston jerked, trying to bat her off. The car swerved several times before he backhanded her, forcing her to let go. But she wouldn't give up without a fight. She jumped on him, causing him to lose control and swerve. He hit her again, knocking her into the passenger's-side window.

The rev of an engine and the sound of a car approaching from behind them caught her attention. Preston gripped the steering wheel even tighter as he watched the car in the rearview mirror. When it caught up with them, Claire saw Matt driving. She screamed his name, causing Preston to shove her back onto the seat and reach for the gun on his lap.

"No!" Claire screamed as he let down the window and raised the gun. She lunged across the seat, grabbing him to keep him from hitting Matt. He jerked the wheel and the car swerved. Her seat belt locked, throwing her backward against the seat. The gun slipped through Preston's fingers as he jerked the wheel. Tires screeched and the car spun out of control. They crossed the lane, clipped the guardrail and careened down the embankment before slamming into a tree.

A blaze of pain shot through her as her head connected with the seat. As she lost consciousness, her last thought was of Matt and thanking God that he was safe.

Matt watched in horror as the car took out the guardrail and rolled down the ravine. He slammed on the brakes, screeched to a halt and was out of the car in a flash. Claire's screams reverberated in his ears along with the cry of metal giving way. Fear gripped him. He had to get to her. He started down the embankment.

"What are you doing?" Ryan yelled. "It's too steep."

"Call 9-1-1," Matt hollered to him and started

down the incline, his only thought being that he had to reach Claire.

Another car screeched to a stop and Josh and Garret jumped out.

"Are you crazy?" Josh cried to him. "You're going to fall and break your neck." He pushed Matt back, blocking his way.

Garrett rushed to the trunk and pulled out a length of rope. "We'll lower you down," he said, handing one end to Matt.

He tied it around him while Garrett and Josh positioned themselves to hold his weight as they helped him descend.

His head was spinning and his heart hammering against his chest. This couldn't be happening again. He couldn't lose Claire this way after all they'd been through. His feet hit the dirt the car had loosened and Matt realized his brothers had been right. He wouldn't have gotten down the steep ravine without falling.

He reached the bottom and called up that he'd made it before untying the rope and rushing to the car. It had landed upside down against a large tree that had stopped its descent. The driver's-side door was open and Matt peered inside. Preston was gone, but blood was on the seat, indicating he hadn't escaped unscathed. But it was Claire who captured his attention as she sat slumped still in her seat by the locked seat belt. Blood dripped from a gash on her head, but otherwise she seemed to be uninjured, at least outwardly. She wasn't moving and he suddenly flashed back to the wreck ten years ago and the terror in her eyes as she pleaded with him.

I can't move.

She began to squirm and Matt breathed a sigh of relief. "Claire, are you okay?"

She opened her eyes, looked at him and flashed him a weary smile. "Haven't we been here before?"

His heart swelled with gratitude that she could still joke around with him. That was a good sign.

"Let's get you out of here." He tried to unbuckle her seat belt but it wouldn't give way. How he wished he had his knife, but Preston had taken that, too, when he'd knocked him out. He searched around the inside of the car for something sharp. He grabbed a piece of metal that had been twisted and dislodged from the window frame and quickly cut through the seat belt. Claire literally fell into his arms and he pressed her to him, thankful for her safety.

"Are you hurt?" he asked her.

She shook her head. "I think I'm okay."

"Then let's get out of here."

He crawled out of the car, then helped Claire out, as well. He held her as she limped back toward the rope where Josh and Garrett were waiting to lift them back up. He reached for the rope, intending to tie it around her, when she cried out. He spun around and saw Preston a few feet away, his gun raised and pointed right at Claire. Matt quickly stepped between her and the gun.

"Nothing good can come of this, Preston. Just put down the gun and let's talk this out." Preston's hand shook with anger and Matt was worried the gun might fire without his intending it to. Matt tried to keep his voice calm and steady as he spoke. "Think about this, Preston. Think about your life and your career. You don't want to do this."

"You're wrong. I've wanted to put a bullet through your eyes from the moment I first saw you. And if Claire doesn't want me, then I have no more use for her, either."

He took a step closer and Matt knew this was no empty threat. "How are you going to explain that you killed two people?"

"Simple. I'll just say Claire died in the wreck and you, overcome with grief over losing her again, shot yourself. I can be very convincing."

"No one will believe that," Matt told him. "My friends are up there. They know I don't have a gun."

"Too bad for them, then. I suppose they'll have to disappear, as well."

"Please don't do this," Claire cried. "You don't have to do this."

Matt knew that wasn't true. He had no doubt Preston meant to make good on his threat. He'd gone too far to go back now. They had to disappear some way so that his secret business could disappear, as well. Even if he had to leave town, he needed time to get away.

But no matter what, Matt knew he had to give Claire a fighting chance. He might not survive lunging at Preston and wrestling him for the gun, but it might be Claire's only hope of escaping.

However, before he could act, Claire lunged toward Preston and the gun. He fired and she toppled to the ground.

He and Preston both stood stunned for a moment at what had just happened. Fear rippled through Matt as Claire pressed at her stomach and her hand came back bloody. Matt tackled Preston before he had a chance to react, knocking him to the ground. The gun fell from his hand and Matt grabbed it. As Preston lunged for him, Matt raised the gun and shot him. He crumpled to the ground and didn't get back up.

Matt rushed to Claire, who was lying still. Blood was pooling around her and her eyes had grown glassy. He recalled that awful night in the car when he'd been sure she was dead. He looked at her now and wondered the same thing. But a soft moan and a slow blink assured him she was still alive.

He picked her up and carried her back to where the rope was lying. He quickly tied it around her and tugged on the line for the boys to pull her up. Once she was safely to the top, they threw the rope back down and Matt scaled the embankment.

When he reached the top, Garrett took his hand and helped him over.

"Where is she?" he demanded, his focus solely on Claire.

"Josh is with her." He motioned behind him and Matt saw Claire on the ground. Josh was beside her trying to keep pressure on her wound. His hands and shirt were already covered in her blood.

"The ambulance is already on the way," Garrett assured him.

Matt stumbled toward her in a daze. This couldn't be happening. Not again. For the second time in his life, he was watching Claire suffer. It wasn't fair. It wasn't right.

His knees buckled and he fell to the ground beside her, lifting up a prayer to God to save her life. "Please, God, help us."

All color had drained from her face. Matt reached

out and took her hand. It was cold to the touch and he recognized the look in Josh's face as he tried to hold back the blood loss. Claire was fading fast.

Her eyes opened and slowly moved to Matt. Her breathing was light and shallow.

He pushed her hair back from her face and locked eyes with her. "You hold on, Claire," he commanded her. "Don't you give up on me now."

Her eyes gradually, methodically closed and her head moved to the side.

Panic ripped through him at the thought of losing her. "Don't you leave me," he told her. "You hang on, Claire!"

The whirl of the sirens approaching them filled him with relief, but when the paramedics arrived and tried to push between them, he refused to release her hand.

"Sir, we need to work on her," a female EMT insisted. "Please let us work."

Josh and Garrett finally had to drag him away and his heart broke as her hand slipped from his. He couldn't lose her now. He couldn't.

The paramedics were busily working on her and they quickly loaded her onto a stretcher and into the back of the ambulance. Matt couldn't tell if she was breathing and no one would give him a straight answer.

The boys stayed beside him as the local police chief questioned him about the events. He was obviously suspicious to have one of his detectives down and he wasn't going to allow Matt to leave until he got answers.

But Matt was determined not to leave Claire's side

even for a little while. He answered the chief's questions curtly. He had nothing to hide but he'd already let Preston get in his way. He wasn't going to allow this police agency to get between him and Claire, as well.

The chief finally had to let them go.

Josh slid behind the wheel before Matt could insist on driving. When they arrived at the hospital, Matt rushed through the halls like a wild man searching for Claire. Thankfully, Josh was with him and calmly asked for directions.

"We're looking for Claire Kendall. She was brought in with a gunshot."

After several excruciating minutes, a man in hospital scrubs approached them and introduced himself as the ER doctor. He explained that Claire was being prepped for surgery to remove the bullet once she was stable enough.

As Matt waited for word, his mind was spinning at all the time they'd lost together. He should have been with her, right from the start, never leaving her. But that was the past and he couldn't change it. As when he was trapped in the basement by Preston, this situation was out of his control. He'd done all he could to save her. Her survival now was in God's hands…as it had truly been all along.

His friends always accused him of being emotionless, and even after the ambush, he hadn't let his grief over his lost friends overwhelm him. He'd kept it tamped down, pushed away so he didn't have to feel it, didn't have to swim in it. Only now he was drowning. All his grief about the ambush and the years he'd lost with Claire came bursting through him, a wave of sorrow such as he'd never experienced. If he hadn't been sitting, he was sure it would have knocked him to the ground. He leaned into his elbows and put his hands over his face and cried out to God in pure anguish.

Josh and Garrett left him alone in his grief, but they didn't leave. When he glanced up, they were both sitting across from him, heads bowed in prayer or on the phone updating the rangers. His family and friends began to arrive, filling the waiting room and joining them in prayer. Friends of Claire's from church and school began to arrive and so did many of her students whose lives she'd touched.

When the elevator doors slid open and the Kendalls entered, Matt knew he had to face them. "What happened?" Mr. Kendall demanded. "We just got back into town. We heard on the news that Claire was shot."

"It was Preston. He shot her."

Mrs. Kendall looked astonished. "Preston's been Claire's friend for years. He would never harm her."

"Well, he did. And he's also the drug dealer who ordered the student killed that she was accused of murdering."

"I don't understand why he would do that. He seemed like such a nice man."

"It's because he thought he owned Claire. He thought he loved her, but the truth is he never knew what true love was. He could never have what Claire and I have."

Mr. Kendall snorted and Matt knew he was about to remark about past mistakes. "I'm not a kid anymore, Mr. Kendall. I love Claire, and I'm planning to stick around this time."

He wondered how Mr. Kendall would respond, but he didn't have to wait for long. The nurse arrived before he could speak to let them know Claire was out of surgery and they could see her now.

"Just family," the nurse said when Matt started for the door.

To his surprise, Mr. Kendall answered before he could. "He is family," he told the nurse, and that was all he said before leading his wife through the doors to see their daughter.

Claire heard murmuring as she awoke. The voice seemed far away but grew closer. Soon, it became clearer and she realized it was prayers. She opened her eyes and looked around. She was clearly in a hospital room, but why? She turned her head toward the sound of praying and saw Matt in the chair beside her hospital bed. His head was lowered and his hands folded in front of him. She heard him whisper her name and realized he was praying for her. Her heart warmed at the sight.

He raised his head and found her watching him. He reached for her hand and softly spoke her name, his mouth curved into a smile and his eyes glowing with happiness.

"What happened?" she asked him, her voice low and raspy.

"You're in the hospital. Don't you remember?"

She searched for the memory but everything was fuzzy. "Prom?' she whispered. No, that wasn't right. That was long ago. Something else had happened to her. And then the memories flooded her. "Preston."

Anger bit through her as she remembered his betrayal. "Is he—"

"He's dead. He can't hurt you or anyone else again."

She closed her eyes and felt a tear slip from her eye. Preston had been her friend once, or so she thought. She'd cared for him, and despite all that had happened, she knew she would have a difficult time getting over his betrayal.

Matt squeezed her hand reassuringly. "I'm here, Claire. And I'm not going anywhere. I'm going to be right here beside you until you're better."

Her heart warmed at his declaration, but Claire didn't miss the "until" he'd added. She shook her head, unwilling to settle for that. "It's not enough," she told him. "I don't want that."

He looked confused and started to pull away, but she gripped his hand tightly. "I want more, Matt. I want you to stay even after I'm well. I want you to promise to stay forever. I'm alive because of you, because you didn't give up on me. Tell me you love me and that you'll never leave me."

He smiled, then leaned down and kissed her face, punctuating each of his words with a kiss between them. "I love you, Claire, and I will never ever leave you again. That's a promise."

Tears sprung up in her eyes as Matt reached for her hand and stared up at her with love gleaming in his hazel eyes...love for her. "I'll hold you to that for the rest of my life."

EPILOGUE

The wedding went off without a hitch. Claire smiled as she watched Alisa and David say their vows to one another before a church full of their family and friends. Claire was happy to be included among them.

A strong hand reached for hers and Claire grasped it, soaking in the feeling of Matt's skin against her own. She was finally home where she belonged, by his side. The nightmare of the past two weeks was over. Ryan had come clean on everything he knew about the Trixie ring operating in town and had cleared Claire of any involvement in Luke's death. Matt had interceded for the boy and got him leniency in exchange for his information.

As the ceremony ended, Claire joined in the fun at the reception. Matt leaned close to her and snapped a picture of them, then kissed her cheek.

"I love you," he whispered. "I never want to be without you again."

She leaned into him. "I feel the same. I love you, too."

He picked up their glasses and stood. "I'll go get us a refill."

She watched him walk away, then scanned the event room. After a moment, Alisa rushed over and reached for her hand.

"I'm about to toss the bouquet," she proclaimed. "Come on, Claire. All single ladies are required to participate."

She tried to wave away the offer. She had just gotten out of the hospital only a few days ago and she was still stiff and sore from the gunshot wound. It had taken great pains just to dress for this event, but Claire hadn't wanted to miss it and her mother had quickly offered to help. Even her relationship with her parents had taken a turn for the better.

"I'll just watch from here," Claire insisted.

Alisa shook her head. "You know if you catch the bouquet, it means you'll be the next one to get married."

She hated to disappoint Alisa, but she glanced over at the line of Alisa's single friends and family members. She'd seen fights for catching the bouquet get ugly quickly at other weddings, and she was in no mood to do battle for it.

But she couldn't deny the pleading in Alisa's face. Matt's family had been kind enough to include her in this special day. The least she could do was join in this harmless fun.

Alisa squealed as Claire stood and walked over to the area where the others were waiting. A semicircle formed near Alisa as she turned and prepared to toss the bouquet over her shoulder.

Alisa tossed it and Claire realized it was coming right at her, but instead of jumping to catch the bou-quel, the women surrounding her stepped out of the way and it landed right in Claire's arms.

The crowd squealed with pleasure and Alisa turned and clapped. "You know what that means, don't you, Claire? It means you'll be the next to get married."

She started to laugh it off, then realized all eyes were behind her. Claire turned. Matt was there on one knee.

Her heart swelled with anticipation as she realized all this had been set up. Tears sprung in her eyes as Matt reached for her hand and stared up at her with love gleaming in his hazel eyes...love for her.

"I've loved you since I was sixteen years old. Claire Kendall, will you do me the honor of finally becoming my wife and a permanent member of the Ross family?"

Her heart overflowed with love and happiness. It had been such a long journey and she was finally able to say the words she'd always longed to say to Matt.

"Nothing would make me happier than to become your wife. I love you, Matt."

He slipped the beautiful ring on her finger, then stood and kissed her as their family celebrated. Claire snuggled closer against Matt and took comfort in the only place she'd ever felt safe—wrapped in the arms of the man she loved.

* * * * *

Dear Reader,

Thanks for reading *Reunion Mission*, the second book in my Rangers Under Fire series. I hope you enjoyed reading Matt and Claire's story as much as I enjoyed writing it.

I love reunion stories! Few things in life are worse than regret. We all have things in our past that we wish we'd done differently, but thankfully ours is a God of second chances. Reunion stories by definition give characters a do-over and who doesn't love that? Matt gave in to fear and shame after the car wreck on prom night and guiltily left town. That decision followed him for years, coloring all of his relationships. His unexpected return to his hometown provided him with a second chance he never thought possible. And while this story may be fiction, the principle is real. God is working every day to redeem our mistakes and provide us all with the second chances we need.

If you struggle with regret from past choices, let me remind you of the promise given in Romans 8:1 that there is no condemnation for those who are in Christ Jesus. Jesus is the great restorer and nothing is better than that.

I love hearing from readers! You can find me online at virginiavaughanonline.com.

Virginia

COMING NEXT MONTH FROM
Love Inspired® Suspense

Available May 3, 2016

TRUTH AND CONSEQUENCES
Rookie K-9 Unit • by Lenora Worth
Army medic David Evans has one goal: track down his late comrade's sister and fulfill his promise to look out for her. But he's shocked to find Whitney Godwin's a single mother and a K-9 rookie cop...with a drug ring's target on her back.

EMERGENCY RESPONSE
First Responders • by Susan Sleeman
When EMT Darcie Stevens is brutally attacked, she has no idea who is after her. But Detective Noah Lockhart is determined to find out who wants her dead—and keep her and the little girl she's caring for safe.

SEASIDE SECRETS
Pacific Coast Private Eyes • by Dana Mentink
Navy chaplain Angela Gallagher and army doctor Dan Blackwater are tied together by the tragedy that took the life of Angela's bodyguard. So when the fallen man's twin brother is in trouble, they rush to help him—and thrust themselves into danger.

PLAIN PROTECTOR • by Alison Stone
Social worker Sarah Gardner flees to an Amish community to escape her abusive ex-boyfriend. But when a stalker brings danger to her new home, can she trust deputy sheriff Nick Jennings to protect her, or will she need to run again?

TACTICAL RESCUE • by Maggie K. Black
When Rebecca Miles is kidnapped by criminals seeking the computer decryption program her stepbrother stole, she's rescued by her former sweetheart, special ops sergeant Zack Keats. But as they investigate her brother's treason, they realize that nothing is quite as it seems.

UNKNOWN ENEMY • by Michelle Karl
College professor Virginia Anderson won't let anything stop her from translating a set of ancient tablets—even attempts at blackmail that quickly turn deadly. But she'll need help from former Secret Service agent Colin Tapping to keep her alive long enough to succeed.

LOOK FOR THESE AND OTHER LOVE INSPIRED BOOKS WHEREVER BOOKS ARE SOLD, INCLUDING MOST BOOKSTORES, SUPERMARKETS, DISCOUNT STORES AND DRUGSTORES.

LISCNM0416

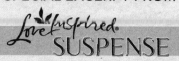
A military medic and a rookie K-9 officer find a connection in the midst of a drug crisis in Desert Valley.

Read on for an excerpt from
TRUTH AND CONSEQUENCES,
the next exciting book in the captivating
*K-9 cop miniseries, **ROOKIE K-9 UNIT**,*
available May 2016 from Love Inspired Suspense.

"Get out of here. Now."

David Evans glanced up at the man holding a gun on him and then glanced down at the bleeding man lying on the floor of the passenger train. "I'm not leaving. I'm a doctor, and this man needs help."

The gunman who had just stabbed the train attendant glanced at his buddy, agitation obvious as he shuffled sideways on the narrow aisle.

David had seen the whole attack from the doorway of his seat a few feet up the aisle. While the two argued about leaving without the packages of drugs they'd dropped, David had hurried to help the injured man.

But before they got away, the two possible drug couriers had spotted David moving up the aisle.

"You better keep traveling, mister, if you want to live. I'll finish off both of you if either of you talk."

David held his breath and stayed there on his knees while the two men rushed off the train.

"I'm a medic," he told the shocked older man. "I'm going to help you, okay?"

The pale-faced man nodded. "He stabbed me."

"I saw," David said. "Just lie still while I examine you. Help should be on the way."

When he heard sirens, he breathed a sigh of relief.

He'd come here searching for a woman he didn't really know, except in his imagination. But a promise was a promise. He wasn't leaving Desert Valley without finding her.

When he looked up a few minutes later to see a pretty female officer with long blond hair coming toward him, a sleek tan-and-white canine pulling on a leash in front of her, David thought he must be dreaming.

He knew that face. While he sat on the cold train floor holding a bloody shirt to a man who was about to pass out, he looked up and into the vivid blue eyes of the woman he'd traveled here to find. Whitney Godwin was coming to his aid.

Don't miss
TRUTH AND CONSEQUENCES by Lenora Worth,
available May 2016 wherever
Love Inspired® Suspense books and ebooks are sold.

www.LoveInspired.com

Copyright © 2016 by Harlequin Books, S.A.

LISEXP0416

SPECIAL EXCERPT FROM

Love Inspired®

*A marriage of convenience for widowed single
parents Joshua Stoltzfus and Rebekah Burkholder
will mean a stable home for their children.
Becoming a family could also lead to healing their
past hurts—and a second chance at love.*

*Read on for a sneak preview of
AN AMISH MATCH by* **Jo Ann Brown**,
available May 2016 from Love Inspired!

"Will you give me an answer, Rebekah? Will you marry me?"

"But why? I don't love you." Her cheeks turned to fire as she hurried to add, "That sounded awful. I'm sorry. The truth is you've always been a *gut* friend, Joshua, which is why I feel I can be blunt."

"If we can't speak honestly now, I can't imagine when we could."

"Then I will honestly say I don't understand why you'd ask me to m-m-marry you." She hated how she stumbled over the simple word.

No, it wasn't simple. There was nothing simple about Joshua Stoltzfus appearing at her door to ask her to become his wife.

"Because we could help each other. Isn't that what a husband and wife are? Helpmeets?" He cleared his throat. "I would rather marry a woman I know and respect as a friend. We've both married once for love, and we've both lost the ones we love. Is it wrong to be more practical this time?"

Every inch of her wanted to shout, *"Ja!"* But his words made sense.

She had married Lloyd because she'd been infatuated with him and the idea of being his wife, so much so that she had convinced herself while they were courting to ignore how rough and demanding he had been with her when she'd caught the odor of beer on his breath. She'd accepted his excuses and his reassurances it wouldn't happen again…even when it had. She'd been blinded by love. How much better would it be to marry with her eyes wide-open? No surprises, and a husband whom she counted among her friends.

She'd be a fool not to agree immediately. "All right," she said. "I will marry you."

"Really?" He appeared shocked, as if he hadn't thought she'd agree quickly.

"Ja." She didn't add anything more, because there wasn't anything more to say. They would be wed, for better or for worse. And she was sure the worse couldn't be as bad as her marriage to Lloyd.

Don't miss
AN AMISH MATCH
by Jo Ann Brown,
available May 2016 wherever
Love Inspired® books and ebooks are sold.

www.LoveInspired.com

Copyright © 2016 by Jo Ann Ferguson

LIEXP0416

Turn your love of reading into
rewards you'll love with
Harlequin My Rewards

Join for FREE today at
www.HarlequinMyRewards.com

Earn **FREE BOOKS** of your choice.

Experience **EXCLUSIVE OFFERS** and contests.

Enjoy **BOOK RECOMMENDATIONS**
selected just for you.

PLUS! Sign up now
and get **500** points
right away!

Earn
FREE
REWARDS
HarlequinMyRewards.com
Join
Today!

MYR16R

Love the Love Inspired book you just read?

Your opinion matters.

Review this book on your favorite
book site, review site, blog or your own
social media properties and share your
opinion with other readers!

Be sure to connect with us at:
Harlequin.com/Newsletters
Twitter.com/LoveInspiredBks
Facebook.com/LoveInspiredBooks

HLIREVIEWSR